SECRETS
of the
DUNES

Also by Julianna Kozma

Mosquitoes of Summer

SECRETS
of the
DUNES

A Hannah and Emily
Morgan Mystery

JULIANNA KOZMA

McArthur & Company
Toronto

First published in Canada in 2011 by
McArthur & Company
322 King Street West, Suite 402
Toronto, Ontario M5V 1J2
www.mcarthur-co.com

Library and Archives Canada Cataloguing in Publication

Kozma, Julianna
Secrets of the dunes : a Hannah and Emily Morgan
mystery / Julianna Kozma.

ISBN 978-1-77087-016-1

I. Title.

PS8621.O979S43 2011   jC813'.6   C2011-902926-X

The publisher would like to acknowledge the financial support of
the Government of Canada through the Canada Book Fund and the
Canada Council for our publishing activities. The publisher further
wishes to acknowledge the financial support of the Ontario Arts
Council and the OMDC for our publishing program.

Cover photograph: Superstock
Typesetting: Kendra Martin
Printed and bound in Canada by Trigraphik LBF

10 9 8 7 6 5 4 3 2 1

To Kira, Emmie, and Daniel.
You make me laugh! Love you to bits.

Nothing happens unless first a dream.

—Carl Sandberg

Prologue

The young man stood on the edge of a rocky red cliff. A strong wind buffeted his long black hair and tickled his golden brown cheeks. His soft leather tunic flapped against his thighs, and the birch bark quiver of arrows strapped to his back moved around with each new gust. A storm was definitely heading towards the island.

He shaded his odd blue eyes against the glare of the afternoon sun and squinted hard, trying to get a better look. He could see something just past the peninsula to his left.

A young girl snuck out from behind a large patch of blackberry bushes and suddenly appeared beside him.

"I found you, Sakima!" she cried happily. "I told you that you can't hide from me forever. I'm the best tracker in our whole village. Grandfather said so."

Sakima smiled as he glanced down at the giggling girl. Except for Sakima's moccasins, they wore similar clothes. The girl's small brown feet were bare and caked with red mud. The only splash of colour on her outfit was a beautiful armband made of bright yellow gold. The green, red, blue, and yellow jewels on the armband sparkled brilliantly in the sunlight whenever she moved.

"That you are, little one," he chuckled. "And if grandfather says you are the best tracker, then that is the truth. But why are you wearing the Spirit Fire? Are you not afraid of losing it while you are playing hide and seek?"

"I wrapped a bandage around my arm and then smeared it with some pine sap," explained the girl. "It was very sticky. Then I put the armband over the wrapping. It is on so tight, I'm not sure I will be able to take it off ever again. So don't worry about your dear old Spirit Fire. In fact, you worry way too much."

The little girl laughed teasingly at Sakima, and then clapped her hands.

"Now then, it's my turn to hide. Let's see if you're as good at tracking me. I will give you a bit of time to find me, since you're a bit slow—maybe till the sun gets to the Pointed Finger Rock—does that sound reasonable, or do you think you will need more time? After all, you're not as good as I am and—"

"I think we will have to play another time, Kanti," interrupted the young man. He turned away from the girl to gaze out at the sea again. "The wind has picked up from the northeast, and the clouds are quickly rolling in. It seems Grandfather was right once again. A storm is building, and it looks like it might be coming straight at us."

"Ooohh, I just love these summer storms," Kanti said eagerly. "Can we stay and watch it from here? Your lookout shelter is still standing, and it looks like most of the pine branches are in good enough shape to keep the rain off of us. Please, please, please. Let's stay."

"No, I don't think so," said Sakima, shaking his head. He frowned. Although he could see white caps out at sea, he was certain that he could see something else. Whatever it was, it would disappear for a few seconds in the troughs between the waves, but then pop back up with each swell.

"Why can't we stay?" whined the girl. She picked up a handful of small stones and threw it over the edge of the cliff. "I'm not a baby anymore. I can stay by myself if I want to."

Sakima glanced down at Kanti and smiled at her, then he looked back out towards the water. He stiffened as he finally realized what it was he saw. And if he was right, it was bad news. Very bad news.

"Kanti, you say that your eyes are sharper than anyone in the village," he said, bending down to where his sister was sitting. "Tell me what you see, just off the Pointed Finger, in the water."

The girl, now intrigued by Sakima's unusual seriousness, stood up for a better look. She focused her unusual blue eyes on where her brother was pointing.

"Quickly now," he urged.

Kanti was surprised to see fear in her brother's look. She turned and looked out towards the sea, her face now matching his in its intensity.

"I see it," she gasped, "or rather them—boats with large white sails—five of them. But I don't understand. What does this mean?"

"It means we are in trouble," he cried. "We need to get to the village as fast as we can. We need to warn the others. Run!"

Within half an hour, the village was in an uproar. People frantically dashed to and fro, carrying overflowing baskets and leather bundles. Campfires were extinguished, and the glowing embers were crushed underfoot. Wooden shelters were denuded of the yellowing skins of drying cod that had gleamed in the late afternoon sun. Youngsters gathered the stone and wooden tools that were scattered around the village. Everything was thrown into a quickly growing mountain of essential belongings.

Sakima stood outside the door of the largest wooden shelter and watched the mounting panic run rampant through his village. He could see the choppy waters of the bay just past the edge of his home. The storm was moving in fast. He turned his back on the scene in disgust, pushed aside a leather curtain and stepped inside the wooden structure.

The interior of the house was very dim, and he needed a few seconds to adjust to the darkness. A shaft of sunlight shone through the smoke hole in the ceiling, and in the reflected light he could see his sister, Kanti, sitting cross-legged next to their grandfather. They both looked very worried. They were quiet until Sakima was seated in front of them.

"So they have come," whispered the old man. It was a statement, not a question.

"You were right, Grandfather," Sakima said,

bowing his head in respect. "They have come as you said they would, and in greater numbers than before. It does not look good."

"Unfortunate, but not surprising," the old man sighed, closing his watery eyes.

"They have come to take what is ours," cried the girl, pounding her small fist against her knee. "We cannot let them."

"We have little choice," the old man sighed again, gently taking hold of Kanti's hand. "They warned us of this the last time they were here. Our waters are rich with fish. They are a treasure for greedy people. We do not understand their ways, and they do not understand ours. We cannot change that. The spirits know that we have tried. We must leave our home once again, like our ancestors did before. We no longer belong here. But we must flee together. Our people, no matter how different we are from the others, must stay together."

The chief turned his attention to the young man again and asked, "When do you think they will arrive?"

"We have perhaps an hour. The storm is blowing them slightly off course, and they seem to be struggling against the force of the waves.

But their boats are strong, and although they are coming in slowly, they are making steady progress."

"Maybe their boats will crash against the rocks and sink," Kanti suggested.

The old man closed his eyes. "I have a bad feeling about this storm. The spirits have not favored us this time around. Our escape will be made all the more difficult by the weather. You must tell our people to abandon things we cannot easily carry. We need to move swiftly if we do not want to get caught."

"They have come for our treasures," continued grandfather. "They will take them by force if they have to—we cannot allow that to happen."

Sakima knew what he had to do. "I won't let it come to that," he said. "I will bury them in the original home of our ancestors."

Grandfather nodded again. "It is a great risk. You need to be quick and leave no trace of your route. These men know what we have, and they want it."

Turning to the girl, Grandfather reached for her hands again and gently said, "Little one, you will need to make this journey without me. I must stay here. I will be the last defense for this village.

If I can delay these invaders long enough, you will have time to make it to the other side of the island. Your brother will follow you after he is done with his mission."

Tears streamed down the little girl's face as she cried silently. She knew there was no arguing with her grandfather. He was wise, and she trusted him, but that did not mean that she liked his decision.

"Will you join us, too—after you are through with the white men?" Kanti sniffed, trying to be brave.

The old man looked at her for a long moment. "The journey will be long, and I will try to come. But remember, I will always be with you—in your heart and in your head—no matter what happens. Go now, before it is too late."

The girl threw her arms around her grandfather, kissed his wrinkled cheek, and got up to leave. Her brother got up as well and followed her out of the building.

"Go swiftly, and do not look back for me," Sakima told her. "I will follow you as soon as I am done hiding our treasures. Go with the other women. Mimi will take care of you. She always respected grandfather's decisions. Our cousins are leaving now, and Mimi is waiting for you. Be safe.

I will see you soon." He gave her a quick hug and turned back into the wooden house.

Kanti was left alone outside. She watched the villagers scrambling to pack. She listened to the muffled voices of grandfather and Sakima. She did not want to go, but she did not want to disobey grandfather either. Still—this was a special case. She wrung her small hands as she struggled with her decision. Then she dashed into the woods behind Grandfather's house where she had a secret hideout up in an old beech tree. She had decided. She would wait until everyone had left before she would come out again. She would stay with Grandfather and protect him.

She looked down at her crossed arms; she was still wearing the jewelled armband.

After leaving his sister, Sakima and the chief had gathered together the sacred objects of the village. This is what the invaders were after. The treasures left to his people by the ancestors had to be preserved at all cost. As he bundled their treasures into the rawhide blanket, Sakima suddenly realized that Kanti was still wearing the armband. He looked frantically around the village and found no trace of her. He would have to leave without it.

Sakima raced through the woods, struggling to hold onto the bulky rawhide blanket. Tree roots made him stumble over the uneven forest floor, and low-hanging branches drew blood as they whipped across his face. Behind him he could hear the horrific sounds of guns, and the faint cries and screams of the villagers who had not made it out on time. He prayed Kanti was safe.

Then... *Boom! Crack! Crash!*

Sakima stopped at the top of a clearing and turned towards the direction of the boom. Off in the distance, past the forest path he had just run through, he saw a rising cloud of smoke. It slowly dispersed to the east as it gave in to the will of the strong wind. His village was ablaze. And the storm had arrived with a vengeance. Thunder and lightning crackled through the sky, and Sakima felt the sharp sting of hail and rain hit his face and exposed hands.

Dismayed at the horrific sight of storm and smoke, he closed his eyes and prayed that grandfather was unharmed. Then with a sigh, he turned his back on the devastation and sprinted across the clearing. He feared the lightning as much as the enemy that might or might not be chasing him. Within seconds he was back inside the sheltered dimness of the woods on the other side of the clearing. His laboured breathing took on a new note of urgency as he raced towards his secret destination.

By late afternoon, Sakima was exhausted. But still he pushed on, keeping up an almost inhuman pace for the next three days. Finally, he neared the sea again. The tangy salt air teased his dulled senses, and a refreshing wind ruffled his sweat-drenched hair as he made his way out of the woods and across the soft sandy beach. The storm had stopped not long after it had started. Perhaps the spirits were finally on their side after all!

Sakima finally came to a stop. He gently lowered his bundle to rest at his feet and gasped for breath, choking and coughing as his lungs struggled for air. Sakima slowly straightened up and looked at his surroundings.

A half-moon had just begun to peak through the tatters of clouds, and it cast a brilliant glow on everything. The beach was almost a twin to the one near his village. It opened out on to the Gulf of St. Lawrence, which at this moment and despite the previous storm, was a calm giant gently lapping at the edge of the red sandy shoreline. Huge sand dunes and rocky red cliffs were sandwiched in between the beach and the forest that Sakima had just run through. They were covered with razor-sharp fronds of grass and looked like lonely sentinels. The mountains of sand provided an effective windscreen for the saltwater marshes that lay just behind them.

With a final deep breath Sakima picked up his precious bundle and started off down the beach. He skirted around the edges of the dunes until half an hour later he came to a rocky outcropping that jutted out from one of the giant sand monsters. He paused for a moment to gather his strength. Then he approached the outcropping, more cliff-like than anything, and started his climb. Halfway up, he stopped on a flat rock and rested a bit, listening. The only sounds he heard were the splash of the lapping waves as they reached the shore. Long gone were the sounds of the invasion of his village.

The rocky path was barely visible in the moon-light, and Sakima turned his back on the peaceful scene and continued to climb again. At last he reached the top, and there, just beyond the end of the path, he saw the dark opening to a cave. It was well hidden. The entrance only appeared to be a small crack in the rock face. From where he was standing, Sakima was almost convinced that he would not fit through the opening, but he knew this was a trick of the eye.

He would need to make a torch to see inside the cave. From within the folds of his tunic he drew out a flint stone and set about lighting a small fire. It was not an easy task since everything was still damp from the heavy rains that had washed the island. He fashioned a nearby piece of driftwood and an old animal skin into a crude torch. Sakima tried to dry out the driftwood as much as possible in the heat from his fire, but he was not sure whether it would work or not. He desperately hoped that it would. When the wood was finally dry, he lit his torch, picked up his bundle and quietly disappeared into the cliff's small black opening.

Thirty minutes passed. Then an hour. The night remained quiet. Sakima finally reappeared, looking exhausted but pleased. He threw down his torch, and it went out immediately as it hit the wet grass.

He had done it! The sacred objects of his village were safe within the depths of this secret cave and only he and grandfather knew where they were hidden. The spirits would lie silent and wait for the day that the people would welcome them back.

Chapter 1

Hair Effects

Teeny One, otherwise known as Emily, sat at the antique kitchen table and stuffed her mouth full of ripe raspberries.

"Whatcha doin?"

Mr. Bean, the family's mustached parrot, screeched from his cage next to Emily.

"These are great, Mr. Bean!" she mumbled, bright red raspberry juice dribbling out of her mouth. "The best I've ever had...yum! Need more! Oops...Do raspberries stain wood? Hmmm. Looks like they do. Do we have any *Nutella*? Raspberries and *Nutella* would go great. Or better yet, chocolate fondue. Let's heat up some... OUCH! MY EAR! You burnt my ear!! Holey moley! I actually heard my skin sizzling."

Gigi grimaced, and quickly put down the hot hair iron. She anxiously looked over at Hannah,

Emily's older sister, who also sat at the table and quietly waited for her turn to have her hair done. "If you continue squirming like a worm, I might even singe your scalp. And the jabbering has got to end. Do you ever stop?"

"Nope! No off button on this chicky-poo! Ain't my life super cool, Auntie G?!"

"For some," Gigi complained. "Now hold still!"

"As long as you're not burning my forehead, then I guess I'm okay with it," Teeny One said. She licked her fingers and then gently massaged her injured ear. "Mom already did a great job giving me a scar there from her own hairdressing attempt last week. I bawled my eyes out for days."

Teeny One's mother raised her eyebrows as she washed dishes in the kitchen. The open-concept kitchen was separated from the dining area by a countertop. This made it easy for Mom to watch her best friend, Gigi, try to arrange the girls' hair for the end of the year school dance. "There! You're done."

"Cutie-pie!" Mr. Bean screeched again.

Emily, also known as Emzolina, or Emzo for short, slid off her chair and hopped out the back door, singing a Christmas tune along the way. It was June.

Mom watched Emily through the kitchen window as she jumped out onto the patio deck and headed down the stairs. She ran straight for a large but evil Linden tree that waited to toss her off its branches...again.

"My kids are freaks," Mom mumbled as she went back to stir a pot of simmering spaghetti sauce.

Gigi, brush still in hand, agreed. She also watched as Emzo pulled herself up the main tree trunk using a piece of broken garden hose as a makeshift rope. As Emily swung her bare feet towards her goal, the momentum swept her past the tree, and she rammed straight into the back fence. However, the bounce off the fence planks was an almost perfect ricochet, and she managed to plant her feet on one of the lowest branches of the tree, seemingly unhurt.

Gigi turned away from the door and sighed.

"There must be an easier way. However, it's sadly clear that Emzos bounce! On the positive side, at least she's not wearing her pretty dress yet. Okay, you're up next Hannah, and considering the poof ball sitting on top of your head, I'm seeing major pain coming your way."

"I don't know...," Hannah said as she slowly

made her way to where Gigi was waving the hot iron around. "I hate having my hair done."

Hannah's dark brown hair frizzed and waved because she had washed it. Mom had asked Gigi to blow dry it straight before she styled it. With mom's round brush in hand, Gigi was doing well until Mom went upstairs to get a sweater. Suddenly the blow dryer clanked to the floor and everything went silent, including the Bean.

Surely a bad omen, thought Mom. She came back downstairs.

Gigi was hunched over Hannah's head, her face set in a horrific grimace.

"What's up?" Mom asked nervously.

"Well, we seemed to have suffered a *wee* bit of a setback," Gigi whispered. Then, after a quick glance at Hannah, she silently mouthed the words: *Her hair is completely wrapped around the brush, tangled beyond belief.*

"Oh, it can't be that bad," Mom laughed as she moved towards her daughter. "Let's disentangle it, bit by bit."

Half an hour later, Hannah was still hunched over the kitchen table reading her book, oblivious to the panic stricken looks that passed above her head with increasing frequency. Mom and Gigi were sweating. Bucket loads.

"Is there a hairdresser around here who could take her?" Gigi asked Mom.

"It's almost six o'clock, and unfortunately they won't take walk-ins." She pulled out another strand of hair from the brush. "Besides, they must be seriously booked—all the girls are having their hair done. This end of the year dance is a big thing."

"And you're missing one important fact," Hannah interrupted without looking up from her reading. "I am NOT going out in public with a freaking hair brush sticking out of my head!"

The women continued working on Hannah. Suddenly they stopped what they were doing, straightened up and looked at each other.

The decision was made.

Mom walked over to a set of hooks near the basement stairs and lifted off a pair of sharp scissors.

"Hannah, we need to tell you something," Mom started. "Unfortunately, we couldn't get all the hair off the brush, so we need to cut the rest off. And it's really close to your head, soooo...you might have some hair sticking out, kind of."

"You mean punk like?" Hannah asked, finally looking up from her reading. "Cool!"

"Wow," Hannah gushed ten minutes later, as she preened in front of the living room mirror. "It really does look great. I think it's a good style. In fact, all fourteen-year-olds should look like this."

"Whatcha doin?" Mr. Bean stood in the doorway of his palatial home and surveyed his surroundings. Several of his toys were scattered across the wood floor and Hannah had to watch where she stepped. As she bent over to pick up some Lego pieces and a dented Barbie head, the bird gave her a wolf whistle.

Then Emily hurtled up the patio stairs, screaming. Tears streamed down her cheeks, and bits of leaves and twigs poked out of her formerly neat hairstyle. Her left knee was smeared with blood.

"The tree hurt me," she wailed. "I'm sure it did it on purpose. I bet I whacked it too hard with the tire swing. How am I supposed to go to the dance tonight looking like this? The bleeding won't stop. I need an ambulance. Again! But no, maybe the doctors will decide to cut off my leg. OH MY GOD! If they do that, how will I dance? Call off the ambulance, Mom! Fix it! ...and can

I use some of your foundation? I need to hide these other bruises on my legs. They don't look so good."

"Neither does your hair," Hannah said as she handed Emily a wet face cloth.

Mom got to work on the knee. After a good wash to take off the blood and the layers of dirt, she could see that the wound was not that bad. The bruises were another story. Emily's skinny little stick legs were covered with a large number of patches of various shades of blue, green, yellow and brown.

"I don't think one bottle of cover-up makeup will be enough to hide all these bruises," joked Mom. "We might need to buy some shares in a makeup company just to deal with your legs. Why don't you consider wearing some pantyhose instead? Beige ones would do a pretty good job hiding this mess."

"But then I'll be hot," Emily moaned. "I hate that. I'm a free spirit, and my legs don't want to be trapped in some synthetic monstrosity called *panty*hose. God! It's like wearing underwear on my legs!"

"Wow, Emily just used a big person word," Hannah grinned. "Way to go, Emzo! There might be hope for you yet. By the way, where in the world did you ever learn the word 'synthetic'?"

"Stop teasing your sister, Hannah," Mom warned. "Either way, Emily, while you decide what to wear, Gigi needs to do some damage control on your hair. Like it or not, you are staying away from that tree for the rest of the day."

"That tree is out to get me! I just know it. It's pure evil. I can hear it planning its next move all the way from here. I need some ice cream. Do we have ice cream? Where's a bowl? Spoon, too. Oh yeah, chocolate syrup. Almost forgot the grated cheese..."

"No ice cream!"

"No ice cream?"

"No. It'll be suppertime soon."

"NO ICE CREAM?!"

"NO! N.O. NO! Now sit down!"

All in all, that was an interesting hair session, thought Hannah. *Oh well, chalk up another not-so-unusual day in the Morgan household.*

She really hoped that her summer vacation would go better than the afternoon had gone.

Chapter 2

The Letter

Summer at last! On their first official day off, Hannah and Emily played outside with neighbourhood friends. Emily avoided being grabbed by the 'Evil Linden Tree'; Hannah went swimming at the neighbours, and both sisters went biking until the sun set. Their parents fired up the gas grill, and all the kids who decided to stick around the Morgan's backyard shared hamburgers and hot dogs. While everyone was seated around the patio table nestled among the cedar trees, Mr. Bean sat on the back deck in his 'outdoor' cage and tried to catch the flies that came too near his orange beak.

Isabelle and her older brother, Nicholas, lived just down the street and were about the same age as Hannah and Emily. Isabelle was a tall, thin and pale girl. "So what are you doing this summer?" she asked Hannah, "We're going to spend the summer with our dad, but we'll come back for a couple of weeks to be with our mom and step-dad. They want to go up north and enjoy the lake."

"We're going to do the usual," Hannah replied in between mouthfuls of hot dog. Ketchup, the only condiment on her dog, was Hannah's favourite and only vegetable. "As soon as mom finishes up all her work here at the house, you know, cleaning and packing, we're heading down to the Blue Lobster, our house in Prince Edward Island."

"You guys are so lucky," Nicholas sighed as he picked up his tall glass of cola. "I loved it when we went to visit you in PEI a couple of years ago. The ocean was really fantastic, especially the waves."

"Yeah, but remember when our step-dad ploughed into Mom when he was body surfing?" Isabelle reminded her brother. "That was not fun. Lucky thing the Smith's were there to help us." Isabelle looked at Hannah to explain, "—we got to stay at their house while Mom was getting patched up in the Summerside hospital."

The Smiths, better known as Alice and Roger, were very close friends of Hannah's family. They lived in Vermont, but spent their summers in Prince Edward Island. Hannah remembered that they had bought an old home almost a decade ago. It was called the Buzzel House and was located in French River, Hannah's favourite spot on the island.

"I remember their daughter, Lucy. She was really nice to us, and showed us around that part of the island," Nicholas said. "She was kinda cute, too!"

Emily made a face. "She's too old for you!"

"Only by a year," he exclaimed. "Besides, I don't mind older women. They have experience."

"Experience in what?" Emily asked, wide-eyed and innocent.

Snort! A huge spray of orange soda came gushing out of Hannah's nose and mouth.

"GROSS!!!"

"EEEEWWWWW! It went *everywhere*!" Isabelle squealed.

"Whatcha' doin?" yelled the Bean, startled by the sudden yelling.

"Sorry 'bout that," Hannah wheezed as she tried wiping the sticky orange mess from her face. "Orange soda doesn't taste so good when it comes out of your nose."

"Oh gosh...everyone...look at Emily," Nicholas whispered.

"Oh my," Mom said. She stopped dead in her tracks with a tray of plates and chocolate cake balanced in her hands.

Emzo glared at her sister. Her beautifully styled hair was dripping wet with orange soda. The curls that had bounced around her elfin face just minutes before now lay in dank, wet waves that glistened in the dying rays of the setting sun. Hannah watched in horror as orange liquid oozed from her sister's forehead and slowly made its way down to the tip of her nose. Hannah instantly knew she had only minutes to live.

"Emily, it was an accident..." Hannah pleaded.

Mom bent down and faced the smoldering Emzo. She spoke slowly in hopes that the message would get through. "Your sister did *not* deliberately aim in your direction. It really was an accident. I'll help you get this cleaned up. Just keep taking deep breaths, and count to ten. Good girl."

Hannah warily watched as her mom pried Emily's fingers off the arm of the lawn chair. Emily's small mouth moved, and Hannah guessed that the mumbles were actually numbers. At least she hoped they were. Anger management techniques were still relatively new in her sister's life. As Emily shuffled her way around the table and into the house, the mumbling continued.

"You do realize you'll regret all this," Isabelle turned towards Hannah.

"No kidding," Hannah said, shaking her head. "What's worse is that I won't know when it's going to hit me. That little thing is sneaky!"

Fifteen minutes later, a calm and dry Emily made her way back to the table. She daintily sat down at her seat, her damp hair pulled back in a tight pony tail. She looked up and smiled sweetly at Hannah. Hannah turned towards Mom in panic.

Bribe. Mom silently mouthed, her face turned away from Emily. *Ice cream. Store. Tomorrow.*

Hannah gave this some thought—bribing Emily was not a bad idea—although Hannah was not too pleased that her sister would benefit from an accident. Just to keep Emily quiet, and so that she would get a chance to live out her life a bit longer, Hannah made the offer. All in all, not a bad deal, Hannah thought, she'd get an ice cream treat, too—a double bonus. Maybe she should snort soda more often!

When everyone was done with the cake, and the shock had worn off, Hannah's Dad came into the house and said he had a surprise.

"You mentioned the Vermont Smiths before..." he paused and glanced at Emily, who continued to smile sweetly. "Anyway, guess who sent you two a letter? Lucy! I have it right here. Hannah, why don't you read it out loud so we can all hear it?"

Hannah took the letter from her dad and began to read.

Dear Hannah and Emily,

How's it going? Isn't it great to finally get away from school? No more waking up early. I really couldn't stand that. Well, you know I've been working on my fundraising campaign...that school trip to Europe is costing me an arm and a leg, and raising the money for it has taken up a lot of my time. Mom and Dad helped me out a lot. We just had a fundraiser this weekend and made about $500 bucks. Not bad! It's going to be my spending money.

Dad donated a couple of his homemade bottles of wine, as well as a bottle of his Mr. Bean Chocolate Orange Port towards my cause. Who would have thought that bird of yours was going to have a wine named after him? Anyway, we sold some raffle tickets with the wine as the prize.

A couple of months ago Hartland had its annual Spring Fair, and we set up a food stand to raise more money. Mom and Dad made up some lamb skewers and barbecued them. They sold like hot cakes. And tell Emily to calm down....It was one of my uncle's sheep. Boo and Surprise are still alive and kicking. Or should I say, 'butting'. Boo is getting to be a handful, and I'm afraid he's turning towards the dark side. He keeps head butting everyone who goes near him. He might not last long in our barn. Sorry Emily.

I leave for Europe in a week, and will be gone for 19 days. We land in France, and the first stop is Paris. I can't wait! We'll be visiting the Louvre and getting to see the Mona Lisa. I'm hoping we'll be able to get up the Eiffel Tower. They told us that the lines were really long and the wait was over two hours just to get to the top. We'll see. I'm also going to Germany, Holland, and Switzerland. So exciting! Wish you were coming too! But I'll be back just in time to head down to Prince Edward Island. And on that note I have a surprise for you guys.

You won't believe this, but guess who I heard from? Remember the mystery we worked on last year about the old shipwreck washing up on our beach in French River? We solved that with the help of Mr. Mackenzie. Well, he promised us some kind of reward, and he finally came through on that.

You both know that as a historian he is associated with all these people who deal with the history of the island. He's actually quite a big honcho in PEI. There's been this big archaeological dig going on in and around Cavendish, as well as out towards the eastern end of the island, near Greenwich. They're looking for and finding all sorts of things, from early Native American pots and arrowheads, to artifacts from the first European settlers on the island.

But listen to this: through his connections, he got us in on these digs. We can help out on the Cavendish dig, and even better, there's this Greenwich Archaeology Camp for kids, and he booked us for a couple of weeks. We're going to help all these experts look for evidence of early life on the island. Isn't that cool?! Maybe we'll even find some buried treasure with all that digging going on. Yeah, yeah, I know...we had quite enough with all this treasure stuff last year and it turned out to be nothing even close to actual treasure. But who can resist the possibilities?

Actually, there have been some rumours flying around about a lost city being buried somewhere along the north shore. The people who built this alleged city are supposed to be real old, dating back even farther than the Native Americans. And Mr. Mackenzie found something that might make this a real thing. Can you imagine us being able to look for a lost city? We might even discover Atlantis! Well, probably not Atlantis since that's supposed to be somewhere in the Mediterranean Sea, but you never know! And oh yeah, Jack—Jack is coming too. Not sure if that's good or bad. So get your gear together.

Take care,

Lucy

Emily and Hannah looked at each other. In a rare moment of complete understanding, they high-fived, hands slapped in unison. Both started talking at the same time.

"Treasure! Again!!"

"Archaeology! How cool is that?"

"We get to see Jack again!"

"Maybe he'll have more ghost stories to tell."

"I'm sure he'll work a pirate angle into anything we do together."

"I need to pack my digging tools."

"I need new clothes!"

"And I need new shoes."

"I love my shoes. But I could always use more. New is good!"

Hannah's Dad intervened before the girls had spent the entire contents of his wallet on a new wardrobe.

Isabelle and Nicholas looked puzzled.

Hannah turned to them, "Last year a part of an old ship washed up on the beach in French River," she began. "After exploring the wreck, Lucy found evidence that someone had been looking for something in that ship. We automatically assumed it was treasure. What else could it have been? That's when we met a boy called Jack. He thought it might actually be pirate gold."

"Of course he would...he's a boy!" Emily said, waving her hand around dismissively.

"Anyway, he decided that he wanted to tag along with us and try to solve this mystery," Hannah continued. "Then stuff suddenly started to disappear."

"...and this strange man kept following us," Emily added. "He looked mean and was always mad at us. We just knew he had something to do with our mystery."

Hannah continued again, "In the end, the treasure turned out to be some valuable papers that dealt with an inheritance, which sucked for us. And the strange man turned out to be a good guy in the end. The papers really belonged to him, and they proved that he was a Lord in Scotland. When he's not in Scotland, he works as a historian here in Canada, in particular in the Maritimes. As a historian, he's into all the archaeological digs out in PEI. I guess this is his way of paying us back for the help we gave him when we found those papers. He's the one who got us in on these cool digs."

"Wow, you guys are really lucky!" Nicholas said. His face was all aglow with excitement. "Maybe we'll be able to visit you at the dig when we come to the island."

The following morning started off dark and rainy. Hannah loved it! It was the perfect weather for indoor activities like surfing the net. After a quick breakfast of chocolate chip cookies, Hannah went back to her messy room and grabbed Lucy's letter off her nightstand. The mention of Atlantis really intrigued her, and she wanted to learn more about this ancient legend. In grade six she studied Greek mythology, and the stories about all the gods and goddesses fascinated her. She scrounged around under the covers of her bed until she finally pulled out a battered looking canary yellow notebook. Another search through a pile of discarded dirty laundry produced a small red laptop computer. Fifteen minutes later her notebook was filled with a couple of pages worth of information on the lost city of Atlantis.

"Whatcha' doing?" Emily crawled into Hannah's room with Mr. Bean perched on her back.

Hannah glanced up from her computer. "Getting some info on Atlantis. I want to know all about it before we get to the island. What on earth are you doing on your knees?"

"The Bean wanted to go for a ride."

Hannah frowned. "He told you that?"

"Yup! We communicate. So, what did you find out about Atlantis? Enquiring minds like mine want to know."

"I didn't know you had one."

"What? An enquiring mind?"

"No. A mind in general!" Before Emily could snap back, Hannah quickly summarized her findings. "Atlantis was first mentioned around 360 B.C. by a guy called Plato. He wrote that Atlantis was swallowed by the sea 9200 years before. It was the city of Poseidon—"

"Greek god of the sea." Emily nodded sagely.

"—yeah, well anyway, as I was saying, nobles and other powerful people lived in Atlantis and used the island's natural resources to become rich. Their power stretched into Europe and Asia. Over time, the people became greedy, and this made Zeus—"

"Head honcho of the gods!" Emily interrupted again.

"—angry, and he decided to punish the Atlanteans by destroying the island."

"Good boy, Mr. Bean," the parrot screeched. Emily stood up, and the Bean thumped to the floor.

"Ooops, sorry Beanie," Emily laughed as she picked him up. "Lucy mentioned that we're going to Greenwich. What does that have to do with Atlantis? I don't get it."

"Not surprising," Hannah muttered as she ruffled through her notebook. "According to the info I googled, Greenwich has had many digs over the years. Archaeologists found that the area was inhabited by many cultures even older than the Mi'kmaq. And before you ask, the Mi'kmaq are Native American, or aboriginal people that lived on the island. Mi'kmaq still inhabit the island on reservations."

"I heard that the Vikings also came to the Maritimes," Emily said.

"The evidence that's been found shows that these cultures in Greenwich were not only older than the Mi'kmaq, but also older than the Vikings, who came about 1000 A.D.," Hannah continued, scanning her notes. "The ancient period is referred to as the Maritime Archaic Age, which lasted from 9000 to 3500 years ago. I'm emailing Lucy all this information, and we'll see what she can dig up. Then we'll compare notes when she gets down to the island."

"That's so cool," Emily sighed. "I can't wait to get down there. It'll be an amazing summer."

Hannah had to agree.

Chapter 3

Jack & Lucy

Hannah woke to a sunny but very windy morning. *Typical PEI weather*, she thought as she looked out the living room window. She watched bits of roofing tiles blow away in the wind. *...and there went something white. Oh, that looked like a small piece of rotted wood, probably from the trim around the roof. Yup, the* Blue Lobster *is slowly falling apart, bit by ugly bit.*

Mr. Bean, excited at the sight of Hannah, tried to fly out of his open cage but landed with a dull thud next to her. She bent and picked him up, then headed off to the bathroom, carrying the bird upside down like a purse.

"Can I flush the toilet?" she yelled.

"NO!" Dad yelled back from somewhere in the basement.

"Surprise, surprise," screeched the Bean.

"I heard that," Dad said, as he climbed back up the stairs. "I'm off to the hardware store in Kensington to get some plumbing supplies. I'll be back soon, and then I'll try to get the water going again."

The continual repairs on the house were annoying. The small blue clapboard bungalow was not in the best of shape. The floor was just bare plywood, the kitchen cupboards were mismatched, and all the walls needed plaster and paint. And just last night the water pump would not shut off. When Dad went downstairs to investigate the high-pitched whining noise, he found that one of the pipes leading to the holding tank was leaking. That meant no bath water for the night. Hannah cringed at the thought of her unwashed hair.

"Where's the Emzo?" Hannah asked as she manhandled the Bean back into his cage.

"There, on the floor next to the sofa," Mom replied without looking up from her grocery list. "She had a rough night."

"Guess she rolled out of bed again, or I should say her sofa bed," Hannah said as she made her way to the small form. Her sister was entirely covered by her purple woolen blanket. With the toe of her blue slippers, Hannah nudged Emily.

"HEY! You got me in the nose," Emzo wailed as she jerked up.

"How did I know where your face was?" Hannah yelled back. "You were covered from head to toe, and I thought I was kicking your feet, not your head."

"Girls, enough arguing, go and get dressed," Mom said. "Who wants to come with me to do the groceries after Dad gets back? I'm making the usual run into Summerside for everything we need to get this place set up."

Hannah seriously considered her options. She loved going into town for the large shopping run. She could visit all her favourite spots. The Dollar Store was THE best place on earth, because she could buy a ton of essential stuff for very little money. And God knows she had very little money.

But Hannah also needed to talk to Lucy and Jack. They needed to discuss archaeological tactics, as well as to take a look at Mr. Mackenzie's discovery. He had promised to come down to the house and meet with them tomorrow. Better yet, he had promised them a surprise!

"I think I'll stick around here this time," she told her mom. "I know how disappointed you probably are, not to have me around to keep you company, but there are some really important things I need to take care of first, like seeing Lucy. Is that okay?"

Mom looked all choked up. Hannah guessed that her company had meant a lot to her mom. *I'll try to go out with her more often,* she thought.

Hannah could hardly wait to see Lucy. She was one of Hannah's bestest friends. As for Jack, well...Jack was Jack. He was an unfortunate part of last year's adventure. But Lucy and even Emily considered him a really important part of their detective agency. *Traitors!* And it certainly didn't make Hannah feel any better knowing that everyone thought Jack was *in love* with her. *Yuck! Jack!*

An hour later Lucy was at the front door, a huge smile spread across her face. For the first time in a couple of years, she had no braces!

"We were just getting our bikes out and heading down to the beach," Hannah explained as she headed out the door carrying a small backpack.

"I'm bringing my notebook, and we can talk about the Cavendish dig down there. We missed out on the beach yesterday on account of Crazy Squirrel Two. We laid a trap for him, but he didn't fall for it."

"Crazy's back?" Lucy was shocked. "But your dad dumped him miles from here last year. He didn't chew up your camper's screen doors again, did he?"

"Not yet," said Hannah.

"He isn't really Crazy One," Emily explained, "but Dad is sure it's an immediate relative."

"We found this new guy in the trunk of our car yesterday," Hannah continued, "and then in the engine this morning. Now it's a vendetta, with man against squirrel. Unfortunately for us, squirrel is winning."

"You can use Mom's bike," Hannah told Lucy. The girls wheeled their bikes out of the ugly green storage shed behind the house.

"BOO!"

All three girls screamed and then, quite by instinct, lashed out at the 'Boo'—Jack.

"OW! ENOUGH! STOP THAT!" he yelled, covering his head.

"Oh, sorry, it's only you!" Lucy gasped.

Finger-combing his short, bright red hair back in place, he said, "Let me try my grand entrance again since you messed it up."

The girls just stared.

Jack walked backwards seven steps, stopped,

cleared his voice, put his headphones back on his ears, and then started doing weird Jack things.

"Hi ya, babes, how's it hangin'?" he said, swaying to a tune from his iPod.

The staring continued.

"What? Did I say something way too cool for you chicklets to handle?"

"Who on earth still talks like that?" Emily giggled. "No one real, that's for sure."

"What do you mean?" Jack kept dancing. "All the cool kids from the big city say hi just like that. You should know, since you fine young things come from a happening town like Montreal. And besides, I saw it on TV on iCarly."

"Jack, get real and deal with the times," Lucy began. "No one talks like that, or at least no one should. I'm pretty sure it's illegal. And iCarly?

"What? It's a great show," he mumbled. "I watch it with my grammie all the time. Hey, wait up."

He hopped on his own bike and followed the girls down Lower Darnley Road towards Twin Shores Campground, with its long sandy beach. Hannah and Emily's family used to be regular customers at Twin Shores, camping there for a month every summer before they bought the Blue Lobster.

"Whoa! This is awesome," Jack gasped when they stopped at the edge of the surf. "The waves are *gynormous* today. Must have had a rain storm a couple of days ago."

"Don't you know whether it rained or not?" Lucy shouted above the crashing noise of the waves.

Lucy glanced at Hannah and Emily, who both nodded, and gave Jack a strong shove that sent him flying head first into the water.

"Why'd you do that for?" he spluttered, trying to sit up in the water. The strong waves kept pulling him back down into the sea.

"And for your information, *cough*, I only got here," he gasped and sputtered, "this morning!" He paused for breath. "My parents dragged me to Moncton to visit Auntie May. We've been there for the past three days."

"Are you staying with your grandparents again?" Emily asked.

Jack stood up and struggled to throw off a long and sticky piece of sea grass that was tangled in his shirt.

"...kinda hard to see what's on my back... where'd it go?" He twisted around and tore at his shirt.

"It's there, in between that palm tree with Christmas tree lights on it and the Hawaiian

Elvis," Hannah pointed. "That's some shirt you've got there. I think you have all the colours of the rainbow on it, and then some. Where on earth did you get such a loud shirt?"

"For your information, my shirt was a gift from Auntie May."

Jack tried to fling the sticky piece of seaweed off his hand.

"She lovingly bought it for her favourite nephew. That's me, by the way! I'm everyone's favourite. I think it's a really rockin' shirt. Bet no one on the island will come even close to owning one just like this. They're very rare."

"No kidding," Lucy smirked. "I don't think anyone will actually want to come too close to that shirt anyway, so I wouldn't worry about copy cats. Are you wearing that to the dig?"

"Huh?"

"Never mind." Lucy shook her head. "Is everyone ready for tomorrow?"

"What's tomorrow?" Jack still had a puzzled look on his pale freckled face.

"Didn't you get my letter?" Lucy asked. "I wrote to you a week ago—about the archaeological dig we're going to be a part of."

"Boy, you're dense!" Jack huffed impatiently. "I just told you—I haven't been home for a few days now, and I never checked the mail. My parents drove me straight to gramp's place, and when I saw that you were there I came right over. Convenient to have a house close to yours, right, Hannah?"

"Yeah...a real blast," Hannah mumbled. "Anyway, even with your pea brain you must remember Mr. Mackenzie from last year?"

"Who could forget," Jack smiled, thinking back to last year's adventures with the girls. "You were so scared in the cemetery that you fell right into my arms, Lucy girl. You too, Hannah. That was soooo sweet it nearly broke my heart. I just knew right there and then that I had to protect you both, even if it meant my life."

Lucy threw up her hands in frustration. "It soon will! Now, can you get back on track, Jack? Focus! Please!"

"Okay, Okay," he laughed. "What have you got up your sleeveless shirt now?"

With a big sigh, Lucy told Jack all about the upcoming digs, both at Cavendish and Greenwich. "Your grandpa must have okayed the whole thing because he told my parents that you were coming. He probably didn't have time to tell you about it, before you dashed off to Hannah's place."

"Wow," Jack said. "You think we might

actually be looking for Atlantis? Imagine that; *Jack makes the discovery of the century*...no... *millennium*...scratch that...*the biggest find of all time!* I'll be rich. I'll be famous! Girls will fall at my feet."

"Jack! Snap out of it, will you?" Emily slapped his arm. "If any girl falls at your feet it'll be because you tripped her. And besides, how can we possibly find Atlantis? It's supposed to be in the Median Sea, not the Gulf of St. Lawrence."

"That's Mediterranean Sea," Hannah sighed. Was there even a Median Sea out there?

"Mr. Mackenzie hinted that he found something interesting that is making this dig even more exciting than usual," Hannah continued as she pulled out her notebook from the backpack. "He said it might have something to do with a lost city. But that's all we know. He'll tell us more tomorrow. In the meantime, we need to discuss what we're bringing with us to the dig. I'm making a list. Any suggestions?"

"An outfit just right for the occasion," Jack said. "It's important that we look the part of archaeologists. We have to be taken seriously."

"I think we should do some research on lost civilizations, not just Atlantis but others." Lucy watched as Hannah took down the information.

"Also, I want to look up some info on the aboriginals who first came to PEI."

"I've got a library card," Jack boasted. "We could go to Kensington this afternoon and check out what they have on Cavendish and Greenwich history."

"And look at archaeology techniques, so we kind of know what people will be talking about tomorrow," Hannah added. "I hate sounding stupid. Okay. Sounds like a plan. Let's mosey."

Kensington boasted a modern and fully-equipped library. By the end of the afternoon, Hannah's notebook was filled with information gathered from books, magazines, and the internet. She loved research and considered herself a real pro.

"So, let's see what we've got," Hannah whispered as they all gathered around a table conveniently tucked away in a corner behind a book shelf. "Emily? I see you have a couple of lines. Impressive, considering you don't believe in reading. Jack?"

"Zippo!"

"What have you been doing all this time?"

"The latest Mario Brothers DS game just came out, and I had to get to the next level," he explained. "I couldn't put it down."

"What are you good for then?" Hannah griped.

"Praise! I'm really good with that," Jack nodded enthusiastically. "You did a great job gathering all this research, Hannah. Simply amazing, and I love you for that. What a woman!"

Hannah glared at Jack but decided it was not worth a comment. "I've got tons of information on archaeological tools and techniques, so we won't be completely lost when we get to the dig site. We can make photocopies, and then you can all have copies to study tonight."

"Yes teacher," Jack smiled. "I love it when a woman takes charge. See? More praise."

Hannah growled under her breath. "Moving on...here's a bit about Maritime history. The Atlantic Provinces were probably inhabited about 10,600 years ago. That's around 8600 B.C. When the glaciers started melting after the last Ice Age, the Paleo-Indians from New England moved into this area. Not much archaeological evidence has been found from this culture, except for some spear points. But these people disappeared with hardly a trace."

"Wow! Just like Atlanteans," Jack gazed at Hannah, who continued reading from her notes.

"Another group of people came here around

9000 to 3500 years ago, which is the Maritime Archaic Age. Some artifacts were found in Greenwich, like stone and bone carvings of birds and whales. Also traces of long houses, like what the Iroquois built."

"Why have archaeologists found so little?" Lucy asked.

"Oh! I know! I found that info," Emily had her hand raised. She cleared her throat and read from her paper. "As the earth warmed up, the glaciers melted and the ocean's water went way up, flooding this whole place. And since this island is made up of a lot of sandstone, many things just crumbled away or were covered by water. This lost culture is probably buried in the Gulf of St. Lawrence. Somewhere."

"So, according to what you just said, we might have a lost city right under our noses, buried under millions of gallons of ocean water," Jack mused as he rubbed his chin. "Interesting. We'll need scuba gear."

Lucy frowned. "Yes, well, how do we tie it to Atlantis? I couldn't find any info on that angle."

"Lucy girl! I'm so glad you asked that question, 'cause I have no idea either! Hannah?" Once again, Jack gazed at Hannah.

Oh, for crying out loud, Hannah thought. "Look, Jacko! It's not a large leap. When Atlantis disappeared for whatever reason—volcano, earthquake, or invasion—it only makes sense that some of the people managed to escape. Since they were known to be amazing sailors, it *could* be possible that some stragglers made their way here, either on purpose or by accident. What do you think Lucy?"

"Hmm. PEI is a long way off the beaten path from their homeland," Lucy said. "I mean, if we're saying that Atlantis was in the Mediterranean, it would make sense that survivors would go to Greece or Turkey, not PEI. How would they get here?"

"Strong or unpredictable currents?" Hannah suggested. "A fluke storm? Tsunami? A driving need to discover new worlds? Remember, they were an advanced society. Anything's possible."

"Aha! You've just said the magic words, Hannah my dear," Jack laughed. "Anything's possible! I think we're in for a treat at these digs."

Hannah smiled, in spite herself. "As much as I hate to admit it, you're right Jack. I can't wait till tomorrow. I just know it'll be amazing."

◆ ◆ ◆

The morning weather report promised clear skies, but all Hannah could see from the kitchen window were dark clouds and strong winds. She hoped the archaeological dig with Mr. Mackenzie wasn't going to be a total washout.

"Why are we always being warned not to bring down inflatable toys or boats to the beach?" Emily asked as she chomped away at some peanut butter, maple syrup and cinnamon waffles.

"Strong winds and unpredictable currents pull lightweight boats off shore, away from the island," Mom explained. "The running joke is that the next stop will be Newfoundland, a few hundred kilometres off to the northeast. Are you interested in a visit, perhaps?"

"I don't think that's a very funny joke," Emily mumbled in between noisy bites. "Sounds like an awfully long trip to me. Not too comfy either. I'd rather go by train instead. At least they serve food. You definitely need food for long trips. *Slurp!* Boy, that's great hot chocolate"

"Trains don't go in water, dummy," Hannah laughed, turning away from the window. "There's no bridge connecting PEI to Newfoundland, and no roads either. You can take an airplane or ferry.

Or you can swim. You're a great swimmer. You might think about giving it a try. And by the way, you have a brown milk mustache. It suits you! Don't wipe it off."

Emily stuck her tongue out at her sister, but the effect was somewhat dampened by the glob of semi-chewed waffle that plopped onto the table.

Not long after breakfast, the Morgan's pulled into Lucy's driveway in French River, about a ten minute drive from the Blue Lobster. The Smith's house was an old but well-tended white A-frame set off with dark green trim and decorative gingerbread moldings. It always reminded Hannah of the famous *Anne of Green Gables* House.

"Lucy's lucky to be living in such a nice house," Emily pouted.

Hannah was thinking the same exact thing. *Scary!*

"Why can't we have a house like this?" Emily continued. "I mean, Lucy's house actually works! She has real floors...and doors on her kitchen cupboards. She even has paint on her walls. When can we have paint on our walls?"

"Yeah, our house is more like a nightmare than anything else," Hannah moped.

Up in the front seat, Mom and Dad exchanged funny looks.

Hmm...was something up? Hannah wondered.

"Where are you going, Dad?" Hannah watched as her dad started walking down the drive.

"To visit Wayne Simpson for a bit, until Mr. Mackenzie and Jack show up."

"Oh no, you don't," Mom said as she quickly grabbed the back of her husband's t-shirt. "You're not going anywhere until you drive us all out to Cavendish. Remember, the kids have a date to dig. And speaking of dates, here comes Jack. Oh, look how cute! He's wearing his safari outfit. Boy oh boy, now that's a whole lot of khaki!"

"Wowzer!" Emily whispered.

"*Wowzer?* What kind of word is that?" Hannah questioned.

"It's short for wow," Emily explained.

"What about the '*zer*' part?" Lucy asked.

"What about it?" Emily ignored her.

"Blonde moment," Hannah snickered.

"Never mind," Lucy said. She turned to face Jack, who had finally made it up the Smiths' steep driveway. Huffing and puffing, he bent over, hands on his knees, trying to catch his breath. His thin body was seriously weighed down by a huge pink backpack that looked about ready to explode.

"What's with the bag?" asked Hannah's dad. "Looks like you packed for a month's worth of camping. I thought this dig thing is only for the day. And pink?"

"Yes, sir, pink. It's the *new* pink, specially made for men comfortable with exploring their feminine side," Jack explained as he pulled up the bottom of his safari vest and wiped his brow. "My mom read about this new trend in her *Cosmopolitan* magazine. Thought she'd give it a try with me. Ordered me this bag online in March, but she just got it yesterday. It seems there was a huge demand for it, and it was on back order."

"Did she order your outfit, too?" Lucy asked, finger flicking the brim of Jack's safari helmet.

"Nah. This belonged to my uncle Henry when he was a kid," Jack said, smoothing out an invisible wrinkle on his pressed shorts. "He was a big game hunter for Halloween when he was twelve. I found this in a trunk up in the attic at gramps' place. I think it's just the right look for today's adventure. You girls are very underdressed to me. Not very academic looking, in my opinion."

Minutes later Bill Mackenzie stepped out of his pickup. Although the kids had not seen Bill for the past year, he still looked the same. A tall thin man, his silver hair shone in the sunlight, and his blue eyes twinkled with delight at seeing all the kids.

"How's it going Mr. Mac?" Jack rushed up to

him and enthusiastically shook his hand. "How's the castle in Scotland? And what's life like as a Lord? Is royalty not the best thing in the world?"

Bill Mackenzie chuckled, trying to pull his hand back from Jack's. "Scotland was just great! Had to do some creative financial things to get the castle back in shape though. Got a deal with the Scottish government and turned it into a heritage site. They paid to have the old building restored to its former glory, and in return they get the money from tours. It's starting to look amazing. I'll show you some pictures of it. Despite the ongoing restoration work I decided to come down to PEI and help out on these digs."

"I heard that you found some valuable thingy during this dig and everyone is very excited about it." Emily bounced up and down in front of Mr. Mackenzie. "What was it?"

"It was a rock!"

"A rock?! What's so special about a rock?"

Emily found a stick and was about to throw it into the back yard when Meg, Lucy's lovable border collie, jumped up and grabbed it out of her hand.

"It's this piece of marble." Mr. Mackenzie snapped open an aluminum case and gently lifted out a small and oddly shaped rock.

"From my research so far, I've never come across any ancient artifacts from the island made from marble," Hannah frowned. "It's not a local stone, is it?"

"You're right Hannah! You've been doing your homework," Mr. Mackenzie laughed. "And what do you make of that fact?"

After a bit of thought, Hannah continued. "I think it means that it had to come from somewhere off island, brought here by another culture. Where did you find it?"

"In Greenwich, buried deep. Some student was digging some test spots in the area for a paper he was writing on Greenwich soil stratigraphy—"

"Stratigraphy?" Emily looked up from Meg.

"Didn't you study the paper I gave you yesterday?" Hannah was annoyed. "Stratigraphy is the study of all the layers in soil. Each period of history leaves a deposit in the soil. You can see these layers when you dig down. If you find something in these layers, you can date the object. The deeper the layer, the older the object. But where was the marble piece found?"

"It came from really deep down," Mr. Mackenzie went on, getting more excited. "There was a crack in the soil caused by some boulders that shifted when a tidal surge washed up on the beach a couple of years ago."

"What are tidal surges?" Emily asked, giving up on the stick but now eying the tennis ball locked in between Meg's teeth.

"Tidal surges are giant waves that come in suddenly, usually during storms." This time it was Jack who did the explaining. "As a purebred Islander, I know all about them. These vicious monsters are powerful and can wash very far up on land. The waves can rip away rocks, carve into cliffs and change the look of our shoreline."

"That's very good, Jack," Mr. Mackenzie was impressed. "In this case, the surge freed up some things that were buried a long time ago. And now we are conducting a full survey of the area to see what else we can find."

"Do you know anything about this piece of marble?" Lucy asked, watching Mr. Mackenzie put the marble piece back in its padded foam case.

"Well, yes I do," Mr. Mackenzie continued, rubbing his hands together in suppressed excitement. "If you look closely, you can see some carvings on it. A stylized sea creature. We sent photos of it out to some experts, and they agreed—this same art style is found on some ancient artifacts found in the Mediterranean area, dating back at least 5000 years ago. How did this marble piece get here? That is the mystery we're trying to solve."

"Was it carved here?" Hannah asked.

"Unlikely, since the marble itself had to come from somewhere else."

"True. I wonder..." Hannah looked thoughtful. "If this piece of marble was brought here by another civilization, then we have many questions. Did these people stay on the island? Did they mix in with the people who were already living here? How much influence did they have? What did they build? How advanced were they? And what happened to them? Did they leave? If so, why?"

Mr. Mackenzie laughed again. "My my, so many questions we can't answer yet."

"If you found this piece in Greenwich, why are we digging in Cavendish?" Lucy asked.

"We know that both Greenwich and Cavendish had ancient cultures living along its shores," Mr. Mackenzie continued. "In the past we found a few artifacts like arrowheads and pottery pieces that were from the same time periods, and looked very similar to each other. That tells us that there were people living both in Greenwich and Cavendish during the same time in history. They probably traded between themselves, and eventually with new colonists."

"So are you thinking—" Jack started.

"—You're thinking that if this marble was found in Greenwich, then maybe the ancients that made it could also have come to Cavendish, since it looks like these two places were connected," Hannah finished the thought, suddenly inspired.

Roger, Lucy's dad, joined everyone in the driveway.

"The kids have been talking a lot about Atlantis," he said. "But has there ever been any proof that North America was inhabited as far back in time as Atlantis was thought to have existed, if it ever did in the first place?"

"Yes, there is! There was an ancient mummy discovered in Nevada, USA, in the 1940s. Back then they thought it was about 2000 years old, but with the new radiocarbon dating methods, they tested the mummy again and found it dated back to about 7400 B.C. About the same time that some people speculate Atlantis was destroyed. And what made this mummy very interesting was that it was wearing shoes that were made of woven cloths. Just imagine! Nine thousand years ago people in North America had the technology to weave cloths on looms. This changed our views about how *primitive* our ancient cultures really were. But was the technology developed here, or was it brought here by refugees from societies that were on the verge of collapse, like this mythical Atlantis?"

"Mythical? Do you think Atlantis ever existed?" Lucy asked.

"Well, that's interesting." Mr. Mackenzie rubbed his chin thoughtfully. "Atlantis is a very exciting story and captures the imagination. Its disappearance is a mystery, and everyone wants to find it. Whether it ever existed or not is still being argued by experts. If it did exist, it was around about 10,000 years ago, and then it disappeared without a trace.

"We did some research on this already," Jack said, quickly glancing at Hannah. "Well, at least Hannah did. She's our information hero! I was kinda busy with Mario and Luigi. Anyway, she told us that the island maybe sank during an earthquake or volcanic eruption. With their advanced culture, the Atlanteans could have sailed anywhere and started up new civilizations elsewhere, including here. And now it's our job to find out exactly what happened!"

Jack grabbed his pack and hoisted it on his back. "Let's go ladies. We have an important job to do in the name of science! Discover Atlantis!"

Everyone laughed, except Jack, who didn't think he had said anything funny. Nonetheless, they eagerly followed him to the waiting cars.

Chapter 4

Really Digging It

Cavendish! Tourist capital of the world! Hannah looked out the car window. *Well, ok, not the world, but certainly Prince Edward Island.*

"Can we have lunch at *Pizza Delight*?" From the back seat, Emily craned her head to get a good look at the restaurant.

"No."

"Why?"

"Because."

"Because why?"

Sigh. "Because we packed a lunch to eat down at the dig site," Mom replied. "And sometimes they serve lunch to the volunteers helping out at these digs."

"Volunteers!" Emily squealed. "I thought we were getting PAID for digging. I certainly don't work for free! The fabric of our society would completely break down if people did these kinds of things for free. Capitalism would be doomed. Our basic economic structure would fall apart, and the world would spiral into anarchy. The stock market would crash, revolutions would break out and communism would reign supreme..."

Stunned silence.

"...besides, I need the money for shoes," she finished.

"I told you we shouldn't let her watch all those *Simpsons* episodes," Hannah hissed. "You're a freaking freak! You memorized that, didn't you?"

"Hidden talent," Emily sniffed. "One among many you know nothing about."

"Freaking scary thought!" Hannah said.

Mom turned to Emily. "Sometimes we do things from the bottom of our hearts. It's called kindness. And archaeological digs don't get a lot of money. They get something called *funding*, but that doesn't cover all the costs of the digs. People volunteer to help out, especially students who are learning to be archaeologists. For free. And society benefits because every time you find something, it tells us about how people lived in the past. Historical information is sometimes more valuable than money because we can learn from the past."

"Bummer." Emily crossed her arms over her chest.

"I wonder what kind of conversation Jack and Lucy are having in the other car," Hannah mumbled.

No comment.

"On another note, it sure is a sad day when we have to drive by *Pizza Delight* without stopping in," Hannah continued. "After all, it's been our tradition to have supper there within the first couple of days that we get to the island."

"We'll consider it for tonight," Dad replied. Hannah knew he loved *Pizza Delight* and therefore purposefully ignored Mom's dirty looks.

Hannah looked out the window as they passed through the heart of Cavendish and finally arrived at the gates of Prince Edward Island National Park.

After a park attendant checked off everyone's names, he let the cars through the main gates without charging them the usual entry fee. Dad followed Mr. Mackenzie down a restricted road. It quickly turned into a narrow path leading east and away from the crowded Cavendish area. Once the car cleared the thicker trees, Hannah got a glimpse of water. She was impatient to get started. Some instinct told her this was going to be unforgettable.

"Can we go swimming?" Emily was impatient, too.

"No."

"Why?"

"Because."

"Because why?"

"Because you're working."

"For free!"

"That's right."

"Double bummer!"

They left the cars in a fenced off lot beside a small wooded area, and made their way along a marked path that ended at a cleared area fronting New London Bay. Just past the parking lot lay the dig. It seemed to stretch for miles. Hannah could not believe the action.

The site itself was marked with bright orange survey ropes set out like a giant grid, much like her math notebook. She watched as people went back and forth from these fenced-off square holes. Some carried buckets filled with sand and dirt which they dumped in a growing heap. Others used giant rectangular baskets to sift through the piles of dirt. Long wooden tables were set up around each activity centre, where people were busy brushing and washing what looked like bits of pottery or rock.

"Wow, a real archaeological dig," Jack gushed, eagerly rubbing his hands on his now wrinkled shorts. "I can't believe I finally get to see one on the island."

"Yes, it's not every day you have something like this here, *and* be invited to help out," agreed Mr. Mackenzie. "There are about twenty people working this dig. Dr. Cyril Williams over there is the foreman for the dig, and you'll report to him. He'll let you know what you'll be working on today. He's a major player in the world of archaeology, and he's hoping that this dig will be the crowning touch on his career. He thinks he's just the cat's meow on anything that is related to archaeology. You need to know about something, you go to him...or me. On second thought, coming to me is better. In fact, much better. Ahem!"

Clearing his throat, Mr. Mackenzie continued. "And just past that there big boulder is Marcie Sullivan. She's the assistant to the foreman and is also the head researcher on this project. She's worked on several digs that have gone nowhere, poor dear, and she's hoping that this one might be the biggie that makes her career. She wants the big bucks and the mega stardom that a major discovery will do for anyone's career. Don't let her meek looks fool you though. Something tells me she might be ruthless to get what she wants."

Mr. Mackenzie laughed. "Oh my, I make this crew sound like a list of bad guys in some *Indiana Jones* movie. Kids, don't let me feed your imaginations too much. You'll end up sleeping with your eyes open."

Hannah followed Mr. Mackenzie as he weaved his way through the maze of holes. She glanced down into each pit, hoping to see someone making an amazing discovery just as she passed by. As she neared one of the larger pits, an old lady looked up and waved. Although it was still early in the day, her face was already grimy with sweat and red dirt.

"Come to lend a helping hand, missy?" she croaked in a raspy voice. "I ain't in too much of a good mood since I cracked my favourite set of dentures in half. Really spoiled my mood for the day, get my drift?"

The cantankerous old woman sounded ancient, and looked even older, thought Hannah. Millions of wrinkles lined her tanned face. Then her pursed lips opened wide to show a startling lack of teeth. Snowy white hair poked out from under a floppy straw hat. Hannah couldn't believe her hat. Bright pink and purple plastic flowers lined the hat's wide brim and sparkled every time she moved her head. A gust of wind suddenly lifted up the hat, and with stubby fingers she quickly reached out and rammed the hat back down.

"Don't you worry 'bout a thing, Izzy dear," Mr. Mackenzie said, stopping to look down at the old woman. "This here is my little gang of helpers I told you about. They were sure useful last year helping me solve my inheritance mystery. Now, if Cyril's okay with the idea, you can have the whole lot of them to boss around inside your pit. What do you think?"

"I can sure use some slave labour," Izzy harrumphed. "Them young'uns from the university don't give a hoot 'bout what I have to tell them. Think they know it all already. Fresh meat is what I need, and this bunch looks just right. Except for this safari bloke. What's he up to? Looking for a rhino on the beach, sweetie?"

"My name's Jack, and I'll be more than happy to be at your service ma'am," Jack replied, stepping closer to the edge of the pit.

"At my service for sure you are, Jackie boy," cackled the old lady. "Isabella Arsenault's my name, and I came by way of the Arsenaults up near Abram Village, heart of Acadian country. Welcome to my pit. Haven't had time to tidy up but who the hell cares... Oops! Been told already twice today to watch my mouth with all these here babies round me. What a laugh! Cursing keeps me young. That and cigars. Which reminds me, Billy, where are those Cubans you promised?"

"Now Izzy, you know cigars aren't good for your health," Mr. Mackenzie started.

"My health!" The old lady stood up straight, all four feet eight inches of her. "For your information, at the age of eighty-two, who the hell cares about health? If I can inhale, it means I'm still breathing. That means I'm still alive! I think of it as a reminder that I'm still kicking around. Now then, are we yapping or working, 'cause I have a lot of digging to do."

Mr. Mackenzie sighed and turned back towards Hannah and her gang.

"Sorry about this, but it seems Izzy has staked her claim on your help," he whispered, glancing back to watch the old lady stomp around in her pit. Every couple of steps, Izzy bent over, stared at the ground, swore and spit. Then with a creak of her knees, she would straighten up and move to another location, still muttering under her breath.

"She's a bit eccentric, but Izzy knows more about archaeology than anyone around here," Mr. Mackenzie continued to watch Izzy. "She used to head the archaeology department in Toronto till she retired. Well, sort of retired, since she's still at it. She was born in PEI and grew up in the western part of the island. She's been all over the world, looking at different native pre-historic communities...best person to have on this dig. She'll fill you in on everything we're doing here."

Mr. Mackenzie turned away and started to walk off, but suddenly stopped in his tracks, turned and headed back towards the kids.

"I forgot to say good luck," he said, laughing. "You might need a bucketful with Izzy bossing you around. Have fun..."

With that, Mr. Mackenzie clapped Jack on the back and sauntered off to meet with Dr. Williams, never looking back. If he had, he would have seen a startled Jack fall head first into Izzy's pit. It was not a pretty landing! Hannah *knew* he was too close to the edge.

"Guess that clap on the back was a bit too hard for our Jackie, he-man that he is!" Hannah giggled, gracefully scampering down a short wooden ladder into the pit. By the time she reached Jack, he was being roughly brushed off by Izzy while she lectured him on keeping the site free from contamination. In between more curses, she explained that coming down head first into a pit could upset the exposed stratigraphic layers of earth. Not to mention what it could do to Jack's head.

"How did you know where to dig?" Lucy asked.

"Well, this site all started with some damned tourists getting lost a while back," Izzy said. "They were camping at Cavendish, and decided to take a stroll out this way. A bit far, but you know them tourists, they're a bit insane."

"A friend of ours calls them mosquitoes, because they're real pests," Emily added.

"Well, I guess I'd have no trouble agreeing with that assessment," Izzy nodded. "Anyways, these particular mosquitoes got lost and stumbled on this bay area. They decided they were hungry, and tried digging for clams. Right here! Stupid idiots! Ain't had clams in this area for ages. But you know how it goes with stupid people. Sometimes they get lucky. They found some pottery shards, or pieces, and some nice arrowheads.

"At least they were smart enough to report it to the park rangers," Jack said.

"Right!" Izzy agreed "Finally got the funding this spring from the government. Jackasses! Such tightwads!"

"And then that marble piece was dug up!" Hannah interrupted.

"Oh, you heard about that did you!" Izzy nodded her head. "Yeah, it sure perked up the government's ears. Gave them a reason to spend their money. Found that thing right by that there tree near the stone outcropping. This entire area must have had a major shift when the tidal surge hit here."

"Usually bays aren't affected all that much by these surges," Jack added. "Guess there's always exceptions. Lucky for us! On another note, why the sandbags?"

"Those are put around the top edges of the pits to help keep things from falling into the pits," Hannah explained. "It was in my notes that I copied for you. This way we aren't introducing anything new in the hole. Only an idiot would trip over them and fall in...oops... No offense, Jackie boy."

Sniff. "None taken."

Hannah nudged her sister. "You see those rows of earth?" she asked, pointing to the walls of dirt that were now exposed from the digging. "All those rows of different coloured dirt mean a different period in history. The top rows, or layers, are the most recent. The lower down we go, the older they get. In this way archaeologists can actually date objects found in these layers."

"You hit the nail on the head!" Izzy nodded. "In our case, the first two layers at the top are quite recent, dating from about fifty years ago."

"Looks like a chocolate layer cake, with the darker lines being the yummy chocolate frosting!" Emily hungrily licked her lips.

"It's always about food, isn't it?" Hannah grimaced.

"At least I eat," Emily snapped.

"Hush now, both of you," warned the old lady. "I ain't gonna put up with this bickering, so zip it. Now then, where were we? Oh yeah, the cake..." Izzy bent down and pointed to a dark, almost black streak of dirt running through the wall in front of her. "This layer is most interesting. According to our dating, we believe this layer is about 1000 years old. We have not found anything in the layers above this. However, when we dug down this far, our lives became interesting. We have definitely found evidence of a pre-historic settlement living in this area."

"Cool," said Hannah. "Like digging for treasure. You never knew what you'll find."

As she looked around, she noticed that the pit was not excavated evenly. There were many different levels.

"I guess we have to dig out this entire area all

the way down to your *interesting* layer?" Hannah asked.

"Ho ho, you hit that one right out of the park, as my gramps was fond of saying," Izzy laughed.

Hannah tied up her hair and got right down to work. Much to her chagrin, Jack was right by her side. She watched him fumble around a bit as he tried to figure out what shovel to use.

"Guess I'll have to show you how to dig, too," Hannah sighed in frustration, grabbing a small trowel out of a bucket. "You never dig straight down with your trowel. Instead, you choose a small spot and then slowly scrape away. Whatever you scrape goes in this here bucket. When the bucket is full it's hoisted to the top and taken away to be screened. That means we put it into this giant sieve, like those you use on the beach for sand. When we shake it, the dirt comes out of the screen part, and if we're lucky something larger than the dirt will stay in the screen."

"But that could take all day," Jack complained.

Izzy cackled, having overheard the entire conversation. "Yup! Ain't life a b—oops, never mind, sweetie! All this takes a damn long time, but it's the only way to make sure we don't break anything valuable by digging higgledy-piggledy."

Four faces looked back at her.

"What're you waiting for?" Izzy barked. "Choose your spot and start digging!"

The morning passed painfully slowly, and the day was getting hotter. The sun, which came out thirty minutes after they started digging, was now shining down directly on them. Over the next few hours, Hannah, Emily, Lucy, and Jack found scores of pottery shards, sea shells from ancient food heaps called middens, carbon pieces from long-forgotten fires, a few beads, and some really nice arrowheads.

"Whoever said archaeology wasn't very physical was a damned good liar," Jack said, wiping his dirty hands on his equally dirty safari outfit. "This is frigging back-breaking work!"

"Jack! Stop swearing," Lucy warned.

"That's not swearing," Izzy laughed. "That's only baby-talk! There's a lot more I can teach this sweetie-pie. By the time he leaves here tonight, he'll put sailors to shame. No one will be able to out-swear him!"

"Great!" Jack bent back down to his work. "That's all I need. A degree in swearing! Won't Mummy be proud?"

At about noon, the site workers stopped all work and headed down to the water for lunch. The area overlooking New London Bay was specially cleared for the excavation team. A kitchen tent battled against the breeze blowing off the water. Rows of picnic tables were lined up near the water's edge. A couple of barbecues belched out smoke, and the delicious aroma of hot dogs and hamburgers hit the kids like a sledgehammer.

"I'm starved," Jack patted his stomach. "I could eat ten hot dogs, at least!"

"What a surprise," Lucy smirked.

"Sarcasm does not suit your pretty face," he replied.

"Huh?"

"Never mind."

Lunch was delicious, but they finished in no time. Then it was back to work. Unlike Jack, Hannah did not mind the hard work. In fact, she thought it was actually pretty neat. They were finding quite a lot of artifacts, and her active imagination was creating a story for each discovery. Besides, all that winter shoveling of her driveway back home seemed to have done wonders for her muscles. This was a piece of cake!

The afternoon sun beat down on the teams, but a refreshing breeze off the Gulf of St. Lawrence soothed irritated nerves. Everyone kept refilling their water bottles and using ice cubes to swipe across their over-heated faces.

Much to Lucy's irritation, Jack kept insisting she fan him with his hat every five minutes. After the seventeenth *no*! Lucy finally hit him.

Aside from the sounds of the summer crickets buzzing in the dune grass, all was quiet as they concentrated on their work.

"HOLEY MOLEY! WHAT THE HELL'S THAT?"

Before Hannah could say anything to Jack about his swearing, Emily had rushed past her sister to see what Jack had found. Lucy was not far behind. Izzy creakily stood up from her crouched position and stomped over in her usual no-nonsense style. With a sigh, Hannah joined the rest of the gang and stood next to Lucy, staring down at Jack's discovery."

"Hot damn!" whooped Izzy, slapping Jack hard on the back. "You've just graduated to the top of the class, young man. Well done. Now, what the hell is it?"

"I think I just said that," said Jack.

"Yeah, I know, but now we have to figure this out, sweetie." Izzy looked ecstatic, staring down at Jack's discovery. A narrow but deep crevice ran along the ground where Jack had been digging. Right next to the opening was a flat rock.

"I came across this rock and decided to clean

it off, and then dig around it," Jack explained, wiping more sweat off his filthy face. "After I removed it I found this hole. It looked more like a crack in the ground. When I shone my flashlight down into the crack, I saw it. Amazing, isn't it?"

"But what is it?" Emily demanded.

"Now that looks to be shaping up to be the million-dollar question today." Izzy shook her head. "I'm afraid I just might not be able to answer it. At least not yet." With a gleam in her eye, she turned to her four helpers.

"Now let's get this thing of beauty cleaned up and out of this damned hole!"

Chapter 5

Old Soul

It seemed like the entire dig team was squeezed around the rim of the pit, staring down at Izzy and her four helpers. Dr. Williams and his assistant, Marcie, were among those trying to vie for front row positions. The eager faces whispered excitedly as they looked down into the excavation pit. Hannah felt very self-conscious with all these people staring at her.

After Izzy cleaned off the top layer of dust, she uncovered the form of a small skeleton. Unfortunately, the skull was crushed into several small pieces, but the rest of the bones looked to be in decent shape.

"It's the skeleton of a child, poor thing," Izzy looked up at everyone. "From the size, maybe about ten years old. It's lying on its side. This slab of rock was positioned over the skull. Can't tell for now what killed it. I'll need a forensic anthropologist for that."

"I also see bits of leather among the bones, with some beadwork woven into the material, probably the remains of its clothes," Hannah noted as she stood beside Izzy.

"Good eye, dearie, but looky here," she pointed. "It's this little treasure here that is really fascinating."

Hannah thought that Izzy was definitely in her element as lead excavator. The old woman was really and truly smiling as she delegated work. Lucy and Emily were in charge of ambient noise— no one was allowed to talk above a whisper. Hannah was given the job of holding Izzy's brush and trowel, and Jack was in charge of dispensing water to the thirsty Izzy. Izzy thought she was the star of the hour, and she was busy photographing the crevice from all angles.

Finally, Izzy handed the camera to Hannah. The crowd suddenly fell quiet.

"Probe."

Hannah jumped and retrieved a long metal wand-like object from the tray of archaeological tools.

"Water bottle."

Jack's turn to jump.

"Get the box ready."

Again, Hannah bounced to attention.

The tension was electric. No one moved. Lucy and Emily sidled closer to Izzy, who was flat on her stomach, arms dangling in the four foot long crevice. When Hannah glanced into the hole, which was no deeper than two feet, she saw something glittering among the small white bones.

"Here it comes," Izzy whispered. Hannah dared not breathe for fear of disturbing the hot-tempered old woman. Izzy was even worse than Emily.

Seconds passed. With a huge grunt of effort, Izzy sat up. Slowly, she raised her right arm. *Wow*, thought Hannah, *this is going to hit the papers like wildfire!*

What looked like pure sunlight, mixed with fire and ice, dangled from the end of the metal probe. It was simply breathtaking.

"Ladies and gentlemen, what we have here is the find of the century, perhaps even the millennium," she wheezed. "Behold an ancient artifact that I believe comes from a lost civilization."

Gasp!

"Izzy, are you sure?" asked a shocked Dr. Williams. "After all, it's difficult to date that on site and without testing it. And how can you tell just by looking at it?"

Hannah eased closer to Izzy and bent to inspect the object that still dangled from the probe. It looked to be a decorative bracelet the size of Hannah's hand, about five centimetres wide with an eight centimetre diameter. The entire artifact looked like it was made out of pure gold. The deep yellow colour contrasted with a number of sparkling blue and red jewels. The bracelet was absolutely gorgeous.

"Are those real?" Emily pointed to the jewels.

"Well, if this comes from the era that I'm thinking of, then they certainly didn't know how to make fake gemstones. At least not that I know of." Izzy peered at the bracelet. "I bet these are gen-u-ine rubies and sapphires."

"It's kinda big for a bracelet," Jack said, looking at his own wrist and then, much to her annoyance, he yanked up Lucy's arm for a closer inspection of her wrist.

"Something that size might be an armband, and not a bracelet," said Hannah.

With a smirk, Lucy flicked Jack in the nose with the upraised hand he was still intently examining.

Hannah looked confused as she stared at the sparkling armband. "I thought ancient cultures of North America made jewellery from turquoise or other local stones, not rubies and sapphires,"

"You're right again. This armband is most unusual for the area," Izzy agreed. "I'll have to consult on this one."

"Consult? Izzy my dear, are you sure?" Dr. Williams asked. "I know just the right person."

"I bet you do, Cyril, but I have my own contacts, thank you very much," Izzy cut him off. "And *they* don't hound me to give them credit for the find."

"Now, now. Calm down, Izzy, I'm sure we can come to an arrangement on this," Dr. Williams laughed. "How about a partnership? After all, we're all here together on this dig, and I am the dig foreman—"

"And I got the funding for this damned dig, so I decide who does what," Izzy finished. "Now, hand me that magnifying glass, Emily, and you, Jackie, shine that flashlight on this armband. There, perfect. You see, Hannah, in between the rubies and sapphires there's this beautiful scrollwork design. I've seen similar designs like that before. Odd though."

"Odd in what way?" Hannah asked. She had her own suspicions. In Kensington, she had scoured several websites and had seen some art very similar to what was on the armband.

Izzy scratched her nose with a dirty finger. "Odd because the design looks very much like those found in Ancient Greece."

Ancient Greece! I knew it, Hannah thought.

"But how did it get here?" Lucy was awed.

"That is the million dollar question, my dear," Izzy nodded.

"I think we just found Atlantis," Emily stated matter-of-factly, voicing out loud what Hannah was thinking about just seconds before. "No one knows what happened to Atlantis. It just disappeared. But what if some of its people managed to escape, and somehow ended up here, just like Hannah said. Maybe another new Atlantis was built over here on this side of the world, and then also mysteriously died out."

Dr. Williams grimaced.

"That's a very far-fetched theory," he said. "Atlantis was mentioned in Plato's dialogues the *Timaeus* and *Critae*, but..."

"Why don't you believe the story?" Emily asked.

"Many people, and I am one of them, think Plato made it up to show what happens to civilizations that get too greedy," Dr. Williams shrugged. "Kind of like a fable. I really wonder if our artifact dates that far back. However, as an archaeologist, I will keep an open mind and see what develops."

"Pluto? But he's Mickey Mouse's dog! I didn't know he could talk, let alone write!"

"No Emily, not Pluto, but Plato," Lucy explained patiently. "He was a philosopher from ancient times. Hannah must have mentioned it to you already because she sent me an email about Atlantis."

"Philosopher? What's that?"

Hannah sighed. Sometimes she wondered why anyone even bothered trying to explain anything to Emily. Guess Lucy was one of those saints or something.

"It's a person who thinks about things," Lucy replied calmly.

"Then he's like me, because I think about things, too." Emily was delighted. "I think about a lot of things. I think about what I'll wear in the morning. How I'll do my hair. Which shoes to put on according to my mood. Why I am so good in gymnastics. Why Hannah is such a klutz. Things like that have no easy answers, you know. You should hear what I can come up with. See, that makes me a philosopher, too! Wow. I'll have to tell Mom."

"Okay! So what's next," Hannah said.

"The first thing is to catalogue this properly, and put it away in a safe place," Izzy handed the probe back to Hannah.

As the day quickly came to an end, Hannah and Lucy helped transfer the delicate bones into a specially prepared crate. With the help of digital photographs and computer imaging back at the university lab, the bones would be re-assembled back into the exact position they were originally found.

Izzy prepared a small wooden crate, stuffing the inside with wads of cotton and tissue paper. She used both hands and gently lifted the armband off the tray. Suddenly, a frown appeared on her lined face.

"What is it Miss Izzy?" Jack bent down next to her. The girls sensed Jack's sudden seriousness and turned towards the old woman. The crowd above them had dispersed to their own stations, so Izzy and the kids were alone in the pit.

"I just noticed this when I picked up the armband," she explained, staring intently at the treasure. "This part of the band caught on my finger as I was moving it. See how it curves, almost hook-like? It looks like it was bent out of shape. And there, just a couple of centimetres from the first hook, is another one. But that one is hooked onto the armband."

"It looks like it can be opened and then re-attached to something else." Hannah was frowning. "May I see it?"

Gently, Izzy placed the armband into Hannah's hands. She slowly turned it over, "Did anyone notice this? There's another set of hooks on the armband. I think this piece of jewellery comes apart into two pieces. And there's a design on it. As you said, Miss Izzy, there's a scrollwork pattern, but that pattern isn't random. It's actually the image of a snake. See, there's the head at the first set of hooks...and there's the tail, just past the second."

"Hot damn, child, you're right! How could I have missed that? Guess these old eyes ain't what they used to be. But I think it's really a sea serpent instead of a plain old snake. See all those wavy lines? That's the symbol for water. It looks very nautical in design."

"But what does that mean?" Jack asked. "And where's the rest of the serpent's body?"

"The rest of the serpent's body is with the second armband," Hannah announced, suddenly very excited. "I think this is one of a pair of armbands, and that the two pieces are supposed to hook up."

"A *second* armband?"

"And where in heaven would we find that second armband?" Jack scratched his head.

"Not in heaven, Jackie! Not in heaven...if there's one place we have a chance of finding the matching armband, it would be in Greenwich!"

"Why Greenwich?" Lucy asked.

"Because that's where Mr. Mac found that piece of marble," Hannah almost jumped with anticipation.

"Made by a mysterious civilization that lived on the island?" Lucy speculated.

"...and then disappeared almost without a trace, just before the aboriginal culture moved in?" Jack was excited, too.

"The timing of Atlantis' disappearance would work, if we think those people vanished almost 9500 years ago," Hannah continued. "Some of them could have managed to make it out here, set up some form of civilization, survived for a few hundred years, and then disappeared again. Maybe they even lived with the aboriginals who came up from what is now the US. Maybe as these new people met up with our *Atlanteans*, they inter-married, and the two cultures blended into one."

"I've never heard about anything like that in my island history lessons," Jack muttered, fanning his face with a trowel.

"That's because we've found very little from this culture," Izzy added. "These people liked to be near the water to fish, so we know their settlements were along the island's shore."

"And PEI is primarily made up of sandstone, a very soft rock that easily comes apart. Anything they built with this stone is now gone. Erosion! Geography lesson! I remember that," Emily piped up.

"One of the few things you do remember!"

"Hannah, be nice to your sister," Izzy warned. "And yes, Emily, because of erosion and rising sea levels, many of the earlier campsites of these people are now gone or under water. Which is too bad. We could have learned a lot from them."

Hannah looked down at the armband now resting in the box. "Whoever wore this armband is now long gone, but perhaps she lives on in this. Studying it for clues will help us recreate her world. An old soul in a modern world. That's the beauty of archaeology—isn't it Izzy—bringing the past back to life? I wonder what this armband will tell us? I can't wait to find out. Who's with me?"

Three hands shot up—unanimous!

Everyone was silent, thinking about what they had found.

"You know what all this means don't you?" Hannah eagerly looked at everyone. "We're going to Greenwich to look for the other armband. And if we find the second one, we just might discover the new Atlantis, or an undiscovered civilization. We'll make history!"

Chapter 6

Ambush!

Hannah glanced back towards the dig. The archaeologists had packed up with surprising efficiency. By the time Hannah and her friends had finished putting away the tools from their dig site, Izzy and Dr. Williams had secured the treasured armband. Izzy left not long after that, followed by the rest of the team members. Only Marcie stayed behind.

Hannah thought this strange. The young woman was always looking at her watch with a worried expression on her face. Izzy, too, had noticed Marcie's nervousness at the end of the day and joked that the girl was probably waiting for someone.

"Marcie's very plain looking, and has no personality," Izzy snorted as she and Hannah walked up towards the cars.

Much to Hannah's disgust, Izzy hawked up a large wad of phlegm and spit it into the dirt between Hannah's feet. *Gross.*

"I seriously doubt she would ever have the gumption of actually dating," Izzy continued. "The only man she has ever shown an interest in is Dr. Williams, and the only reason for that is because he looks like her father, who I knew *intimately* in my previous life. Know what I mean?" She winked at Hannah.

That thought disgusted Hannah even more than the spitting. *Was there no end to Izzy's grossness?*

Hannah wondered what Marcie was up to. She definitely looked as if she was waiting for someone. And you never knew with the quiet ones. Sometimes they could surprise you. Hannah saw that the waters in the bay were calm. The area looked very peaceful after this afternoon's exciting discovery. A gentle breeze blew through the dune grasses, and the sharp green stalks swayed slowly in an undulating dance. Every once in a while small streams of red sand cascaded down the dunes as sea birds or crabs looked for food and dislodged the tiny grains.

"That looks like a deep-sea tourist tour boat coming back from an afternoon," Jack pointed out. He shaded his eyes from the sun and watched the approaching boat as it made its way home to the wharf in New London.

"Look! That guy just threw a whole bunch of fish guts over the side. He must be cleaning the day's catch. That's why he has all those seagulls following him. Free food! Which reminds me, I'm hungry!"

Emily ran to her parents' car. "Mom! Dad! We found Atlantis...or at least maybe we did... kinda...anyway, we're going to be famous!"

After an extremely hard day at work, the kids were going to be treated to *Pizza Delight*. According to Hannah's dad, there was also going to be a BIG announcement. Hannah was dying to know what that was all about.

"Atlantis, eh?" Dad muttered, looking a bit distracted. "Sounds cool. That's that legendary island that sank, isn't it? Hope you know how to swim."

"Huh?"

"Never mind."

"Right! Let's go get some pizza." Emily jumped in the car and patted the seat next to her. Within moments everyone was safely belted into the cars and headed away from the site.

As she glanced back for one more look, Hannah noticed Marcie again. *Oh*...She was no longer alone. A very tall man was with her, standing close. Marcie was doing a lot of talking and the man was listening closely, his head almost touching Marcie's. They were too far away for Hannah to make out the man's face, but for some reason he looked familiar. Maybe Izzy's joke was turning out to be true after all, and Marcie *was* waiting for a boyfriend. Boy, Hannah could hardly wait to tell the old woman she was wrong! On second thought, maybe she should think about it first.

Pizza Delight was a Morgan family institution.

Once inside the restaurant Hannah realized she was starving! The delicious smell of garlic bread drove her crazy. She could hardly wait to eat. What was taking so long with their order?

"May I please have your attention?" Dad stood up and tried to get everyone to look his way. "I have an announcement to make. Hannah and Emily—your mother and I decided to surprise you. You know how we have been having problems with the Blue Lobster?"

"You mean the bugs?"

"The leaking pipes?"

"The splinters in the unfinished floor?"

"The mismatched kitchen cupboards?"

"No heating system?"

"No bathroom walls?"

"I see you got the picture," Dad continued. "Well, there were all those problems, as well as the fact that Andrew, with whom we bought the house, has not been the nicest person to deal with. In fact, he wants us gone and has bought us out."

"WHAT?!?!? But then we'll have no house in PEI!" Hannah cried. "Where will we stay? Will we camp again? If we camp, then we can't bring Mr. Bean. What will happen to us? This is terrible. It's not fair?! Oh, my life is ruined!"

"Hannah, stop pulling an Emily. Take a deep breath and listen." Mom patted Hannah on the arm, trying to calm her down.

"Well, because of this unexpected problem, Mom and I have been looking at other houses." Dad looked at Hannah. "In fact, we started the search in February, but we didn't tell you guys because we didn't want to get your hopes up. So... you will not be homeless. Our new house is Just Peachy."

"I'm glad it's just peachy, but what's it really like in terms of looks, location, and things like that?" Hannah questioned.

"No, no...the house is called Just Peachy," Mom laughed.

"Hey, isn't that the cute little green house

next to Wayne Simpson's place, down in French River?" Emily jumped up at this, spilling her water. "I remember, Mr. Wayne told us about it. It belonged to a woman named Peach. That house has so many trees. I can't wait to climb them. When do we move in? And are we still going to go to the Twin Shores beach to swim? Lucy goes there all the time, so we should go as well. Right?"

Sigh.

"I'm going to miss the Blue Lobster," Emily sniffed. "I had a lot of fun in that house."

"Of course you're going to miss it," Hannah crunched on some garlic bread. "You would miss a cockroach if you lived with it for even a few minutes. You just can't let go."

Emily wrung out the spilled water from her napkin and put it back in her glass. Then she picked up her glass and took a sip. Putting it back down, she eyed Hannah and asked, "So what's your point?"

"That was it!"

"What was?"

"You can't let go, Emily."

"Can't let go of what?"

"Of everything, Bozo Brain!!!"

"Idiot!"

"Stupid dummy!"

"Dumb bunny!"

"Twit Brain!"

"Moron."

"Fascinating!" said Jack.

"Creative!" said Lucy.

"ENOUGH!" Hannah's Mom slapped her palm on the table.

Hannah woke to the ringing of the phone. In the suddenness of morning, she was not quite sure where she was. Just Peachy? Wait a minute...she shook her head to clear it, and opened her eyes. *There*, that helped a bit. *Dang it*. A black beetle crawled up the wall. She was still in the Blue Lobster.

The entire space was a mess. Her bed was surrounded by transparent garbage bags. The kitchen cabinets, still without doors, were now almost empty. The area rugs that had been used to cover up the bare and splintery plywood floors were now tied up in rolls and resting against various walls. Several taped up boxes were stacked in the corner of the dining area just opposite Mr. Bean's cage, their contents written out in large black letters. The Bean was hopping on his perch, clearly excited by the mess.

"Mom, I thought you were only moving our

stuff once we'd gone to the Greenwich archaeology camp," Hannah complained, in between bites of one of Mary's Bake Shoppe cinnamon rolls. "And we're going there on Saturday. Today is only Tuesday. What's with all this packing?"

"Change of plans," Mom mumbled as she continued rooting through the upper cupboards.

"Andrew left a message on the answering machine last night, but we only checked it this morning. He's decided to come down and help us pack. Sounds considerate, but his real motive is to make sure we leave our stuff here for him to use. And since *we* brought most of the kitchen dishes, pots and pans, carpets, and linens down here, we are packing them up so that he can't get his grubby little fingers on them."

"Oh, how pleasant," Hannah choked on the roll. A visit from Andrew was definitely no fun.

"When will he be arriving?" Hannah grabbed Mr. Bean out of his cage.

"Andrew said he'll be down on Thursday, but since he lies as often as he breathes, that could be today or tomorrow," Mom said. "Over the next couple of days we're going to make several car runs and move all our things. We want to be gone by the time he gets here, or at least have our things out by then."

Six hours and seven moving runs later, Hannah and her Dad pulled into the Buzzel House's driveway. "We're not staying long, Hannah," warned Dad. "Just saying *hi*, and *how are you*, and then we're off. Got that?"

As soon as Hannah's car door slammed shut, Lucy and Meg came dashing out of the back door and down the patio stairs.

"HANNAH!" Lucy pulled up short, almost bashing into Hannah. Trying to catch her breath, she sputtered out her news. "It's just terrible! I can't believe it. Something like this...how could it happen? I don't understand..."

Hannah took her friend by the shoulders, looked her straight in the eyes and spoke calmly, "Lucy...What the hell are you talking about?"

"Our precious armband was stolen!" Lucy wailed. "Izzy just called. She tried to reach your house as well, but no one was answering."

"When did this happen?" Hannah wailed back. "Does Jack know?"

"I don't know, and yes, Jack knows," she gasped as she sat down on a nearby rock.

"But what happened?"

"According to Izzy's frantic phone call, the armband had been safely packed up before everyone left the dig site. The bones were packed separately and taken by one of the student interns. Izzy herself had certified that the armband's box was sealed properly. It was witnessed by Dr. Williams and Marcie. Then Marcie herself drove it to the University of Prince Edward Island and had it locked up in the archaeology department's vault. This morning, a representative from the Department of Communities, Cultural Affairs and Labour visited the university to catalogue the treasure formally."

Jack and his grandfather had arrived as she spoke.

"Who is this 'communities' person?" asked Jack.

"Izzy said that these guys are the government honchos that are in charge of all archaeology on the Island. The department manages the sites, protects archaeological digs, and gives out permits. You have to be really nice to them or else they won't let you dig. Naturally, they need to know what you discover...like, right away. Marcie was there when this person arrived, and she was going to show him the armband. But when she opened the vault, our treasure was gone! Both Marcie and this government guy looked through all the shelves, but there was no sign of it. All the other bits and pieces that we found yesterday were accounted for, including the skeleton. But no armband."

"Who would take it?" Hannah asked. "This is terrible. No! Worse! This is a disaster!!!"

"What's worse is that the police are now involved, and we're all going to be questioned!" Lucy shook her head in disgust.

"Wow, that's really cool!" Jack eagerly rubbed his hands together in anticipation.

"What? That the RCMP guys are going to question us?" Hannah looked at Jack.

"No! That things are this exciting! So, when?"

"When what?"

"When are we being questioned?" Jack asked.

"Tomorrow," Lucy told Hannah.

Then she turned and smacked Jack on the back of the head. "I can't believe you're enjoying this. Anyway, we're all supposed to head back to Cavendish so that the police can question us on-site. They want us to walk through the packing up and all that. You know, recreate the scene of the crime."

"*If* that was the place," Hannah added. "After all, it could have happened at the university."

"Well, wherever it happened, the detective work starts tomorrow." Jack beamed at Hannah and Lucy, and asked, "Are you in?"

Both girls turned reluctantly towards each other. "What do you think?"

"It might be fun..."

"Maybe...as long as we keep Emily out of trouble."

"Of course! We'll watch the Emzo like a hawk."

After waving goodbye to Lucy and Jack, Hannah and her dad drove back to the Blue Lobster. As they pulled into their driveway, they noticed another car parked near the front of the house. Emily came dashing out from behind a spruce tree, gesturing frantically.

"Andrew's here!"

"Crap!" Dad slammed the car door just as Andrew sauntered outside. He was very tall, thin but wiry, with thick bushy black hair and dark eyes. He wore faded blue jeans and a black sleeveless t-shirt that had an evil-looking pirate on the front of it. Andrew loved pirate lore, and his motto in life could well have been *grab what you want, even if it belongs to someone else.*

"Came to stake my claim on my house," he smirked. "...was disappointed to find you still here."

"The girls were working on an archaeological

dig, and we fell behind schedule," Dad explained, looking up at Andrew. "Besides, we had an agreement."

"Yeah, so what? It's my house now, I can come here whenever I want, like it or not." He turned to Hannah and looked her up and down. "I heard about that dig of yours. Seems you found something valuable. A golden treasure! Right up my alley. Something worth plundering!"

Hannah turned to Emily, who shrugged her shoulders but looked guilty.

"When did you get here?" Dad asked.

"Been on the island for a few days now," Andrew said, scratching his stomach. "I was busy setting things up. I decided to move down here permanently. Gonna develop my landscaping business on the island. I already have clients booked for the summer."

"Yeah, well good luck with that," Dad snorted.

Andrew ignored the jab and turned to Hannah. "So how's the dig going down in Cavendish?"

"How'd you know where we were digging?" Hannah asked. "Did my big-mouth sister tell you about that, too?"

Emily quietly faded back behind the spruce tree.

"Nah! She clammed up after telling me about the armband. News came via the gossip mill. It's a small island. Everyone's talking about it. I find the prospect of treasure fascinating."

"I bet you do." Hannah turned away from him. "Sorry, but I don't have time for anymore small talk. It would seem I need to pack. See you later."

"Oh, I'm sure I'll be seeing you around," Andrew agreed. "As I said before, it's a small island."

Chapter 7

Twenty Questions

Andrew decided to let them stay in the Blue Lobster one more night, but Hannah's dad refused the offer. He suspected that with Andrew there might be strings attached. Instead, the family threw their remaining belongings in the car and left Andrew to his own devices. The following morning, Hannah woke up in Just Peachy.

Hannah loved her new house. Her bedroom window looked right over the wharf in French River, and she was within walking distance of Lucy's house. The light green cedar shingles were beautiful; there was a huge bay window in the front, and several large trees scattered throughout the one acre property. Inside, it was surprisingly big and cozy. Both Hannah and Emily had their own rooms. There were also two spacious bathrooms, and a kitchen with matching cupboard doors!

Bonus! Hannah was impressed. Her parents had made an awesome choice.

After a quick breakfast in their sunny new kitchen, they left for Cavendish. Unlike the first day of the dig, today's weather was dismal. High winds, part of life on the island, were now joined by lots and lots of rain. By the time Hannah, Emily, Jack, and Lucy got together, the dig site was a muddy mess. Small rivers of rain water ran through the entire area, and they quickly developed into small lakes. Hannah noticed that the sandbags that Jack had tripped over a few days ago were now holding back these mini-floods from the square pits. Someone had also covered all the exposed pits with yards of blue plastic tarps, keeping the flooding to a minimum.

"Mighty fine weather we're having, eh missy?" Wayne Simpson laughed as Lucy tried to open an umbrella. Wayne was French River's 'mayor'. He knew everything about French River, and he happened to live right next door to Just Peachy. Lucy's parents had asked him to bring Lucy to the dig today. Hannah knew that he enjoyed more than his fair share of teasing the girls! His short grey hair was smartly covered by a straw cowboy hat that kept most of the rain away from his face.

"Dang it, I forgot my fluffin' fishing rod back at the house. Bet I could have caught an entire boatload of mackerel in that there pit alone. My fiancée, Fanny, would sure have loved frying some of that fish up for Hannah! What ya choking on? Ho! Jacko! Where'd ya come from?"

"Darnley, sir!"

"Nice shirt! Like the silver studs! Mafia boss going out of business?"

"No sir, Walmart special."

"Special my arse," Wayne spat.

"Well, gotta go. Have a great time, my duckies. Get splashing!" Wayne splashed through the muddy rivers, heedless of the splotches of red that splattered the back of his jeans. He waved goodbye to the kids and met up with Hannah's parents back at the car. As the kids approached the first pit, they noticed that their parents were quickly joined by Dr. Williams and Marcie in the parking lot. Even from where she stood, Hannah could still hear Wayne griping about the weather.

The rest of the crew arrived slowly. Many walked around the dig site, inspecting the damage brought on by the heavy rain.

"What a horrible turn of events," exclaimed a voice right next to Hannah and Emily.

Startled, they turned to find Marcie standing next to her. She was dressed in a shiny black raincoat and bright purple baseball cap, with no umbrella to keep the rain away. A steady stream of rain dripped from the brim of her bright cap. Hannah held back a laugh at the sight. Marcie reminded her of a wet cat. But why was Marcie here with Hannah, and not the rest of the grownups?

"The police should be here by now," continued the young woman, oblivious to the drenching rain. Hannah was quite surprised that her usually plain and expressionless face was now flushed with emotion. Hannah wasn't sure if Marcie was excited or angry. "They're always late. Bad habit, that. You need them...you call...and then they take their time coming. Miserable creeps!"

"Are you all right?" Emily asked. "And I don't think you should talk about the police like that. They're like gods, you know, and they'll hear you and then boom, you'll be arrested! Or worse..."

Not for the first time, Hannah wondered how on earth she could be related to Emily.

Marcie nodded to the youngsters. "I'm just very upset by this whole thing. Imagine how shocked I was when I found the shelf empty and the armband gone! That was a historic discovery that would have given our university worldwide fame. Imagine finding an artifact from Atlantis right here on our little island, and we can't even protect it for one day! I don't know what we'll do now. This definitely isn't good news for the dig. Our sponsors will be very upset and might even pull out if that armband is not found quickly."

"Damn right they will," Izzy spat, newly arrived and accompanied by two huge RCMP officers. "We need to solve this mystery and fast. Girl, you better do some talking!"

Izzy wore a bright yellow plastic slicker and matching sailor hat, and Hannah noticed that she eyed Marcie suspiciously. Surprisingly, Marcie did not back away from Izzy's glare. Instead, she completely ignored Izzy and turned to the police officers, shaking each man's hand in turn while she introduced the kids.

Hannah glanced at Izzy. She wasn't the only one who thought Marcie was acting oddly. Izzy, in fact, looked downright confused with this new and improved Marcie. The old woman stared at her colleague very closely for another minute. She squinted through the rain with an evil gleam in her eye. Izzy shook her head in sudden disgust, cleared her throat and then spit...this time close to Marcie's feet.

Officer Hayward, the taller of the two men, told everyone to follow him. The police had quickly set up a makeshift shelter with some extra blue tarps they had found lying around the site. One of the wooden camp tables was placed under the tarp and several wooden crates were scattered around the table. Hannah assumed these were their chairs. Officer Hayward's partner, who introduced himself as Perkins, sat down and opened a battered old notebook. Without a glance at anyone, he ordered everyone to sit down, too.

Oh boy, thought Hannah, *one of those!* She had a feeling that this was going to be a very trying question period.

"Who first discovered the object in question?"

"That would be me," exclaimed Jack, standing up proudly. "Then my humble assistants helped me get it out of the sacred ground and bring it into the world that we live in—OUCH! What was that for?!"

"Jack, do have a sit down on your brain and shut it," Lucy whispered.

"How many people handled the object?" Officer Perkins continued, ignoring the exchange.

"After removing it from the ground, I examined it myself, with gloves, of course," Izzy explained. "None of the kids, except for Hannah, actually touched the armband. And even then it was only for a minute or so. Lucky thing she had a look, because she noticed the sea serpent design that I had thought were only spirals. It seems I need to get my eyes checked. Never thought age would catch up with me. Any who...where was I? Oh yes. Dr. Williams took a look at it as well right before I put it in its box. Marcie Sullivan was with us, but she was just observing. I then placed the armband into the box—"

"Describe the box," Hayward interrupted.

"Oh, I'm good at that!" Jack stood up. He was quickly yanked back down again by Lucy.

Izzy continued. "The cursed box was made of stainless steel, and measured a square eight inches by eight inches."

Hannah remembered that it was brand new and looked sleek, something that a spy would have in his arsenal.

Snapping back to the present, she listened as Izzy continued. "The top of the damned box had a combination lock with a clasp. Only three people had the combination: Dr. Williams, Marcie and me!"

Izzy explained how she placed the armband inside the folds of cotton wool, under the watchful eyes of pretty much the whole dig crew. Then the box was closed shut, and the combination lock spun. A taped seal, similar to ones used to close doors at crime scenes, was then wrapped around it, as added security. The tape would have had to be cut before the box could be re-opened. There was no other tape, because Izzy kept the rest of the tape locked up in her equipment chest. Finally, Izzy had placed the box within a safe from the archaeology department. It was often used to transport valuable objects.

"Did you bring the armband to Charlotte-town?" Perkins asked Izzy.

"No, that would be me," Marcie replied, eager for her turn. "I was put in charge of driving it down, along with Charlie Goodman."

"Were you the last to leave?" said Hayward.

"All the staff was gone by then, but Charlie and I had to wait for the kids to leave," Marcie explained, glancing at Hannah. "When I saw them drive off with their parents, I went to the van where Charlie was waiting, and we left right after that. Before you ask, the armband was never out of anyone's sight."

Hannah stared at Marcie. Why had she left out the part about waiting around for that guy she was with? Hannah knew that the tall stranger was not Charlie Goodman. Charlie was a short man, barely reaching five foot six. And he had red hair, unlike the dark-haired stranger.

Lucy nudged Hannah in the ribs, one expressive blond eyebrow lifted in question. Hannah knew that Lucy had also noticed Marcie talking with this stranger before they had left that evening. Strange that Marcie didn't mention it today.

"Charlie and I had an uneventful ride back to town, and we went straight to the university," Marcie continued. "We drove the van into a special parking bay reserved for staff. It lets us bring in artifacts that we find straight into the storage room. This is a sheltered area, protected from bad weather. We don't want any of our finds being damaged as we remove them from the trucks. I then opened the safe—"

"Was it still locked?"

"Yes and there were no signs of tampering," Marcie continued. "Charlie can vouch for that. I took the box out of the safe and together we brought it into the storage room and placed it on shelf B9, reference number 228. That shelf was reserved for discoveries from the Cavendish dig. All the other objects that we found that day were already on the shelves, in various buckets and trays, awaiting the cataloguing process."

"Did you take the armband out of the box to put on the shelf?"

"No. We wanted the armband to be safe, and the safest place for it was in the locked box itself." Hannah could see that Marcie was beginning to wilt from all the questions; maybe she realized she might be one of the main suspects.

"Who knew that the armband was going to be there?"

"I guess everyone did," replied the young archaeologist. "It wasn't a secret. We just followed standard procedure and placed it where all other finds go."

Perkins turned to Hayward. "Go find this Charlie guy and ask him to come join us"

Minutes later, a cheery-looking young man was shown in and directed to sit on the last remaining crate. When he was asked the same questions, Charlie's version matched up with Marcie's.

"So when you took the box out at the university, it looked just like it did when it went into the van's safe in Cavendish?" Perkins asked.

"Yup!" Charlie agreed. "When the Marsh-mallow—oops—sorry, Marcie, it just slipped out. I talk too much when I get nervous."

"That's okay, Charlie. I knew about the nickname. No biggie," she sniffed.

"Anyway," he continued. "When Marcie took the box out, it was okay. The clasp was still closed."

"And what about the seal? Still in place? And was it in one piece?" Hayward asked, leaning forward.

"Yup, that was there, too," Charlie smiled, enjoying the experience and not in the least bit nervous. Hannah had a feeling that his slip about Marcie being called Marshmallow may have been deliberate. She didn't seem to have many supporters.

"And it was still whole," continued Charlie. "We carried the box inside and put it on the shelf with all the rest of the stuff we found that day. Marcie and I both walked out together, and she locked the door behind her. That's the whole saga."

Izzy spit again, but didn't say a word.

"Did the object in question ever leave your sight?" Perkins asked, frowning at the impossible situation.

"Nope! Once it was put into the van, I sat and waited till everyone left, and it was just me and old Marsh, I mean Marcie, left. We drove off, dumped the armband, and went home. The theft must have occurred after we were gone. You do know that there are security cameras, both inside and outside the storage room."

"Yes, we checked those already," Officer Hayward sighed. "Both you and Marcie were recorded arriving, bringing in the box, and then leaving a few minutes after that—empty handed."

"Then the theft had to have occurred after we left," Marcie repeated Charlie's words.

"And that is where the mystery comes in," Hayward said, slowly shaking his head. "If we believe the security tapes, no one went in after the two of you left that night. You two were the last ones recorded on the tapes until the theft was discovered by Izzy this morning."

Silence. Izzy sniffed. Still no word from her.

"Maybe whoever took the armband played around with the video camera," Jack suggested. "You know, like we see on TV. They stick a photo of the scene in front of the lens so you think you're seeing what is there, but in reality someone is sneaking in and stealing the treasure."

"We don't know what happened yet, but we'll certainly have experts looking at the tapes." Perkins slammed closed his notebook, slapped it against his leg a couple of times, and then stood up, his six-foot-four frame towering over the others. "Thank you for your cooperation, and we'll be in touch when we have further questions. It goes without saying you are asked not to leave this island."

With that warning, he and Officer Hayward turned and left. Marcie, looking paler than usual, followed quickly on their heels. Charlie sauntered out right after her.

Hannah looked at Izzy, who seemed deep in thought. "What's your take on this?" she asked Izzy.

"We need to find out when the armband really disappeared," Izzy began, jumping to her feet. "If it happened after it was already in the storage room, it could be damned near anybody. We'll know more when that tape is analyzed by the police. But if it happened before the armband got to the university, then it has to be one of us."

"You mean an inside job?" Jack exclaimed, clearly excited at the idea. "Oh! This is getting tense! I can become a suspect. Imagine me a bad guy. Girls just *love* it when us guys are real bad! I'll finally have a life!"

"Sucks to be you don't it," Emily cut in. Turning to Izzy, she continued, "But Charlie said he never lost sight of it after you put it into the safe in the van. That would mean he's lying. I like Charlie."

"I know someone who is definitely lying," said Hannah. "It's Marcie. She never mentioned to the police that there was a man with her, here at the dig site."

"A man?" Izzy asked, clearly puzzled.

Hannah went on to describe what she had seen before leaving that evening. "I didn't get a good look at the guy's face. The sun was wrong. But I could still tell that they were pretty chummy."

"Chummy? You can't mean boyfriend like?" Izzy looked doubtful.

"Well, they were standing close together, and I saw the guy actually take Marcie's hand and hold it for a long time," Hannah explained. "As Dad was driving away it looked like the stranger bent and gave her a kiss, but it was hard to tell because the car was moving, and we were too far away."

"I've known Marcie since she first came to the university, and she has *never* had a boyfriend," Izzy snorted, still not completely on board with the idea. "She's been at this dig constantly. I don't see how she had time to meet anyone. That guy was probably a tourist. I wouldn't worry about him. And I know for sure Marcie had no boyfriend before we started this dig because she was always moping around the university, morning, noon, and night. In fact, Charlie made it his mission to get her a man so that she'd stick around less often."

"I'm still wondering why she didn't mention the fact that there was someone here with her," said Lucy, tapping her upper lip in thought. "Unless she didn't want anyone to know about him...and Charlie never mentioned him either. Either Charlie never saw the guy, or he's sharing their secret. Considering what you told us about Charlie, and how he felt about Marcie, I don't think he'd keep their secret."

"Yeah, but did you notice, he left pretty much the same time as she did after the police talked to them...coincidence?" Jack mused. "*I* think not!"

"*I* think we need to talk to Marcie," Emily decided, and ran off before anyone could stop her.

"Great!" Hannah cried in frustration. "Why can't my sister ever think before she acts?"

Hannah left the tent to look for Emily. The police were still milling around, asking questions to the other crew members. The rain had tapered off to a drizzle, and Hannah saw that her parents and Wayne were down near the water. Black cormorants looked for fish, and with the tide low, three Blue Herons stood out in the bay, near her parents.

"I don't see Marcie or Charlie," Jack panted. He had run off ahead of the others to look for them and subject them to more questioning before Emily got to them. "And Marcie's car isn't in the parking lot. I don't know what Charlie drove in with, but I saw no signs of him either. Sorry."

"Well, I'll either see them at the university, or in Greenwich, whichever comes first," Izzy sighed.

Hannah thought the old woman looked depressed. Her swearing quota was way down! That was a bad sign. Hannah guessed that after you had spent a lifetime digging up treasure and finally found one that was truly amazing, it would be hard to accept its disappearance. Izzy waved goodbye to everyone and set off towards her car, a gorgeous fire-engine red Mini Cooper, complete with racing stripes. Typical Izzy!

Back at her own family's car, Hannah got a glimpse of movement from within. Emily was sprawled on the back seat, playing with her Nintendo DS. Hannah eased in next to her, thankful to be out of the rain.

"Did you find Marcie?" Hannah asked, in between bites of a chocolate bar she found squished between the back seat cushions.

"Nope!" Emily answered, without looking up from her game. "Dr. Williams said she left and took Charlie with her."

Hmm, thought Hannah. Either both Charlie and Marcie were in on something together, or Marcie was keeping an eye on Charlie, making sure that he never mentioned anything about that stranger she was with.

Suddenly, Hannah took a good look at Emily's bright yellow t-shirt and black sweats. Absolutely nothing wrong with that. They even matched. A bit bumble-beeish, but that was beside the point.

"Weren't you wearing something else?" she asked her sister.

"Yup, oh observant one," Emily said, still not bothered to look up from her game. "I changed into an extra set of clothes in Dad's trunk. You know the saying, never leave home without it."

"Why did you change?"

"Cause I was wet and dirty."

"So? Since when are you not wet and dirty?"

There went Emily's tongue...and was that a finger? No, it couldn't be. She wouldn't dare!

Chapter 8

Greenwich

Hannah knew that there was something odd about Marcie's story, but she couldn't figure out what. She couldn't wait until the weekend when she'd be in Greenwich.

The last few days had been filled with accidents, and Hannah didn't think that Emily would live long enough to make it to Saturday. While the family was enjoying a hot summer day at the beach at Twin Shores, Emily had snuck off to the campground's play area. The monkey bars beckoned Teeny One, who decided to accept the invitation. She promptly lost her grip on the bars and fell face first on a bed of pebbles. The nosebleed was impressive, the cut above the eye horrendous, the split-lip already swollen, and the screaming unbearable.

On Friday Emily decided to build a tree house.

She designated an ancient Manitoba maple in the backyard as prime real estate. She hauled wooden planks up by rope and strategically placed them on some of the larger branches. Then she hammered them in place. The howling started in the late afternoon.

Hannah explained to Emily that she had to hammer the nails, and not her thumb. When missiles flew at Hannah from above, she decided to stop offering advice. That evening Emily's left thumb was heavily bandaged, and she walked with a limp into the kitchen.

"Why the limp?" Hannah dared to ask.

"The tree threw me out," Emily mumbled. "It let go of the rope."

"Could it be you never tied it properly?"

Emily glared.

"Never mind," Hannah wisely left the room.

As Emily soaked her bruises in a hot bath, Izzy called the house and asked for permission to let the girls stay for two weeks at the dig in Greenwich, instead of the one week that had previously been booked. Hannah's parents okayed the extension, and the sisters eagerly packed their bags on Friday night.

Saturday! Finally! All the bags were hauled into Dad's car, and the mini archaeologists tried to get dibs on the window seats. Greenwich was a good hour's drive from French River. Scrunched in between Hannah and Jack, Emily decided a song was in order. It was never too early for *Ninety-Nine Bottles of Beer on the Wall*.

"I'm looking at the map that Izzy gave us, and I think we're going to be working along the north shore and the Gulf of St. Lawrence," Hannah turned the map on her lap to look at it more closely. "There's this big body of water called Bowley Pond, which has a very long floating boardwalk across it that takes tourists out to the beach. Right next to the beach is the famous parabolic dune of Greenwich."

"What does parabolic mean? Emily asked.

"The sands shift all the time," Hannah explained without looking up from the map. "The dunes look different one week to the next. Very rare in North America. But we're not going to be near this. Instead, we'll be working on the other side of the pond, to the west of the boardwalk. There's another bog pond not far from it. See, Izzy's mapped it all out for us."

"It looks like an awfully long walk from the parking lot to the dig site," Emily complained. The car stopped in one of the park's car lots, and everyone got out.

"Don't worry, Emzo," Mom said. "Look over there. Izzy and Dr. Williams are waiting for you with electric golf carts."

"Now Jack won't get his nice pink bag all dirty," said Hannah. "We certainly wouldn't want Jack to drag it all the way to the camp would we?"

"Certainly not," laughed Lucy. "That would be bad for his macho image, wouldn't it Jackie?"

"Pink is the new black," replied Jack. He jerked his heavy pink bag from the trunk of the car, stumbled with it over to one of the waiting golf carts and took a seat beside Dr. Williams.

"What on earth happened to you, pipsqueak?" Izzy asked as she caught her first glimpse of Emily.

"Lots! Where do you want me to begin?"

"Don't...please," Hannah begged. "This could take all day. Let's save it instead for scary stories around a campfire, okay?"

Everyone laughed, except Emily. Hannah noticed that the poor dear had a hard time with any facial expressions, what with all the swelling and bruising.

Goodbyes, hugs, and kisses were exchanged, and then the amateur archaeologists were off.

The carts made their away from the glimmering pond and along a sandy path that ran parallel to the majestic dunes on the left and the woods on the right. Minutes later, they reached Camp Greenwich.

"Welcome to Greenwich Ground Zero." Izzy swept an arm around the place.

Large multi-coloured tents were spaced evenly around a central space where Hannah could see the remains of a campfire. Some of the tents were bigger than others. And there, in the nearby woods, what were those? Ah yes, more tents!

"Wonder where we'll be sleeping?" Lucy asked, gazing at the hive of activity around one of the tents.

"You girls will be bunking with the rest of the female staff," Izzy replied, pointing towards the bright blue tent off to the left. "That tent can sleep fifteen people, but there'll only be twelve of you. Marcie decided to pitch her own tent out there in them woods...good riddance."

Hannah wanted to ask Izzy about the armband, but Izzy continued giving directions.

"Jackie will be sleeping in the yellow one

down there, just beyond that great old oak. That big but hideous green tent is our science hub. That's where we have all our satellite equipment, computers, monitoring and recording devices, storage compartments...you name it; we have it! This dig is entirely self-sufficient and modern. You kids'll have a blast."

"Where are the other kids who are coming to this camp?" Emily looked around the set up, but saw no one even close to her age.

"No kids."

"What?"

"No kids."

"No kids!"

"That's what I just said!"

"But this is a camp! We enrolled in an archaeology *camp*! WHERE ARE THE KIDS?" Emily was getting frantic.

"No kids." Izzy repeated.

"WHY?"

"Now that's a much better question. You four young'uns are here as a favour to Mr. Mackenzie. Otherwise, we were just fine with the kids from the university. Think of yourselves as privileged. You've gone where no kids have gone before."

"And where's that?" asked Emily

"Here!"

"Hope this isn't going to turn out to be another *Jurassic Park*."

"Emily...they had dinosaurs in that."

"And death! Lots and lots of it!"

"I don't get your point," Izzy shook her head in frustration.

"No big surprise there," Hannah mumbled under her breath. "Many people don't get Emily."

Emily gave Izzy a mean look and spoke slowly. "Those poor kids in the movie were given the same old song and dance about privilege and stuff, and that they should be happy being the first to try out Jurassic Park. Look what happened to them. They became dino-bait. Appetizers before the main meal. Delectable morsels. Tidbits of yumminess. They had to run for their lives throughout the movie. I don't run."

"They made it out alive!" Izzy argued.

"Barely..."

"It's the end that matters," Izzy shrugged her shoulders.

"I'll keep that in mind when the werewolf starts chasing me tonight because of the full moon."

"What are you talking about, Pipster?" Hannah

couldn't believe how Emily's mind worked. *Oh boy*, she thought, *this is starting off just swell*.

Once they were settled in, Hannah and her friends joined Izzy at the main supply tent. They were given identical tool kits filled with various items necessary for the upcoming dig. They got one standard four-inch trowel, plumb bob to make sure the walls were straight, foam kneepads, an eight-metre measuring tape, paint brushes, a set of calipers for small objects, a magnifying glass, comfortable gloves, a whisk broom, small ceramic tools and dental picks, and a horde of black rubber buckets.

Izzy explained how all their discoveries were to be catalogued. "The artifacts will be recorded as they are discovered, but everyone will need to make detailed recordings at the end of each day. The artifacts will be sketched or photographed by the site's archaeological photographer. All buckets with shards and other finds will be labelled with waterproof tags and some placed into labelled plastic bags for separation purposes. Any questions?"

"Miss Izzy, when do we start?" asked Jack, his hand raised high above his head.

"Now. Way over there," Izzy pointed.

Everyone gazed in the direction of her finger.

"I don't see anything," Emily complained. "Where are the pits?"

"Well, we haven't started that many of them in this location," Izzy explained, reluctant to continue.

"But..." encouraged Lucy.

"So what are we working on?" Jack was getting worried.

"Well," Izzy paused. "I think it's better if I show you. You'll get a much clearer picture. Follow me, my little chain gang."

"Hey, weren't chain gangs prisoners or something," Jack asked.

"Guess you can look at it that way," Izzy mumbled under her breath.

They followed Izzy through a small wooded area of beech and elm trees that quickly opened out to a clearing overlooking the Gulf of St. Lawrence. Unlike most parts of the Greenwich shoreline, this area was rockier and more densely filled with vegetation. Hannah noticed bunches of wild lupines growing alongside sea lichen, wild rose bushes, and stunted pines. The wind was sharper here as well since the mountainous dunes were behind her and could no longer afford any protection.

Just off to the right of the path was a hive of human activity. Hannah recognized many of the university students who had helped out on the Cavendish dig. They were now in Greenwich. A handful of pits were already dug, all at varying depths. Mounds of red earth mixed with rocks were piled in several spots around the roped-off dig sites, and some of the students were busy sifting through this dirt, making sure they didn't miss any artifact that could have remained hidden within that red mound.

"See that there beautiful spot, me inmates?" Izzy pointed to a very messy looking outcropping of earth and sand. "That is your little piece of heaven for the next two weeks. It's got your names on it."

"Where?" asked Emily, not impressed. "I don't see anything except a pile of dirt, rocks, and green stuff! Where's our names, and where's the pit?"

"You're making it," Izzy promptly spit in the red sand at her feet. "You have the honour of breaking ground. After we surveyed the area, we picked out certain spots that we think showed signs of past habitation. Usually they're mounds that kind of stick out from the landscape. Other times they may be depressions. This one looks like it's a mound."

"Great...a mound of earth!" Emily mumbled, kicking at the offending dirt. "It's a long cry from Atlantis."

"You never know what's underneath all this," Hannah explained, sweeping her arm across the uninviting pile of dirt and ocean scrub. "Okay! Let's get to work."

"Your optimism is sickening," Emily griped.

"Your face is sickening," Hannah shot back. Not waiting for a reply, she stormed off after Izzy. After some instructions, the kids finally set to work, sweating and digging, digging and sweating. It was painstaking work, but as Hannah said, "You never know what you'll find."

Hours later, Marcie joined them at their site. She started to advise them on which area of their grid they should focus on. Hannah noticed that Marcie was looking a bit under the weather. Her mousy brown hair was a mess, and several strands slipped out from a hastily made ponytail. Her light blue t-shirt was wrinkled worse than Izzy's face, and her jean shorts were stained by who knows what. Hannah recognized that this was not Marcie's usually neat attire. Even the Emzo had commented a while back, asking Hannah how on earth could Marcie keep clothes so clean when playing in dirt all day long!

Never afraid of speaking her mind, regardless of whether it was safe or not, Emily plodded ahead. "Boyfriend dumped you?" she asked, giggling as she handed Marcie a trowel.

"Don't have a boyfriend," mumbled the young woman, looking even more miserable.

"Sure you do! We saw you talking to him back at the Cavendish site," Emzo continued, ignoring Hannah's warning shot. "You even kissed him! Yuck! That was really *gross*."

"I really don't know what you're talking about," Marcie snapped.

"After everyone left, we saw you with this tall, dark haired guy," Jack jumped in. "It's okay. I mean, everyone can have a boyfriend. Even you. Nothing to be embarrassed about. Unless you have something to hide. Do you? Maybe you broke up with him? Things like that happen. Look at me! Girls are always breaking up with me. They just can't appreciate a good thing when they see one. And that guy looked a bit too shifty anyway. A bad influence."

"You kids are terrible." Marcie stood up and slapped the dirt off her knees. "Why don't you just concentrate on the job you were hired to do and mind your own business? I don't have a boyfriend, and I did *not* meet anyone at Cavendish.

You probably saw Charlie. He and I were the only ones left. Why don't you ask Charlie? He'll tell you there was absolutely no one else there except us. And even though everyone loves dear old Charlie Bones, he's not as innocent as you think he is. Everyone has a dark side."

Marcie jumped out of the small pit and stormed off back to the main camp, wild hair flying behind her.

"I think she's mad," Emily said, wiping her drippy nose with dirty hands. Among other things, the Emzo was cursed with hay fever.

"The two of you really upset her," Hannah said, shaking her head. "Can't you at least try to be subtle when you ask people questions. Now she'll be suspicious."

"You can only be suspicious if you're feeling guilty about something," Jack said. "What do you think she's feeling guilty about?"

"I don't know," Lucy frowned. "But she sure wants us to suspect Charlie instead of her. The question is: what does she suspect we know, or think we know?"

"Huh?" Emily now ran damp and dirty hands across her forehead. "I don't know anything."

"We know," Hannah chimed in.

"I think we need to keep a close eye on both Charlie and Marcie." Lucy turned to Jack. "You're sleeping in the same tent as Charlie, so it would be easy for you to follow him around."

"Marcie, however, is a problem because she's sleeping in her own tent out in the woods," Hannah added. "We'll have to take turns with her. And we can't be seen. She's already on to us, and if she's a part of this mystery of the missing armband, then she's going to be much more careful. We need to be really good."

Izzy came to survey their progress at the end of the day. "Three more days of this backbreaking work, and you'll be ready for the real stuff."

Everyone groaned.

"Real stuff?" Emily looked up from her mud pies. While the rest of the kids were cleaning up, she was enjoying the cool feeling of squeezing mud through her fingers. "Isn't that what we were doing today?"

"No honey buns, or should I call you muddy buns," Izzy grimaced. Emily looked like she needed a good soak in the ocean; maybe several hours worth. "You need to get down to a certain level before we find artifacts associated with the timeframe we're dealing with."

135

"How far down do we have to go for the Atlantis time period?" Lucy asked.

"Too frigging damn far," said Izzy.

"We need to find some underground caves or something," Hannah said. "If we look at a period almost 9000 years ago, then any evidence of it is now probably underwater. And this is a big coastline."

"It would be like looking for a damned itty bitty needle in a fluffin' haystack," Izzy snorted. "A search like that would take too long and way too much money in getting underwater equipment. What we need to do is narrow the search area by finding artifacts. Once we do that, then maybe we can convince someone to give us money or equipment for a bit of underwater archaeology."

"Like the armband in Cavendish," Emily exclaimed choking on some accidentally inhaled mud.

"Exactly," Izzy continued, thumping Emzo hard on the back.

"So why are we not digging or doing underwater excavation in Cavendish?" Jack sat down next to Emily. "Why are we here, instead?"

"It takes time to get the permits for things like that, lovey. And we've been digging in Greenwich for a while now, and have found quite a few objects that look promising. I'll let you take a peek later, since you're special," Izzy winked at Jack. "These finds showed us that Greenwich has been occupied during many time periods, or ages. We want to see if we could find remains of their settlements. So far, no damned luck."

"Well, I guess tomorrow is another day," Jack yawned loudly. "Who wants to go for a swim?"

They all did...including Izzy.

Boy oh boy! Izzy in a bathing suit! Hannah thought. *What a scary sight that will be!*

Chapter 9

Nightly Visitations

The next day, Hannah woke up to a dull and overcast sky. She took a few minutes to jot down some details of yesterday's work in her notebook before heading out for breakfast.

The girls were already sitting by the campfire, trying to get rid of the early morning chill coming off the sea, when Jack shuffled over. His arms were extended from his sides, and his knees ramrod straight.

"What's up with you?" Lucy laughed at the spiked strands of red hair sticking up all over Jack's head. He had several scratches on his left cheek. "Had a rough night?"

"Yeah, you could say that," he coughed. Smoke, blown by the wind, rushed right for his face.

"Next time, ask me to spy on someone who doesn't have bladder problems, okay? Charlie got up four times during the night! And he chose different spots in the woods to go visit each time. The last time he went out, the lucky tree was quite a ways away. That last trip out was a killer. I forgot my flashlight back in my tent. I managed to make my way out without any accidents and hid behind a rock and waited. It took a while."

Jack stopped and sat down heavily next to Lucy, cuddling close to her. *Smack!*

"Hey! I was just trying to get warm," he yelped, rubbing his arm.

"That's what jackets are for, Jacko!" Lucy went back to toasting a piece of bread on a roasting stick, watching the flames lick at the edges of her toast.

"...so nothing happened." Emily said in between bites from her bacon and eggs.

"Are you kidding?! Everything happened," he cried, throwing his arms up in the air. "Ouch! Boy I'm sore. After Charlie was done and started heading back to his tent, I turned to follow him. That's when I met up with this blackberry bush."

"Ouch, those are thorny," Hannah said, nibbling on the chocolate she had carefully peeled off her Mae West snack cake.

Jack pointed at his cheek. "That's where I got these."

"Your knee seems to be oozing something, too." Lucy frowned as she looked down at Jack's right knee. A wet spot was coming through his pant leg.

"And I got that tripping over a tree root near Marcie's tent." While Jack was talking he rolled up his khaki pants to investigate the oozing knee. A large area of skin, the size of a quarter, had been scraped off. Bright red and still wet, the injury looked painful.

"Why were you at Marcie's tent?" Lucy asked.

Carefully dabbing his knee with a napkin from Hannah, Jack continued his story. "You're probably wondering why I was at Marcie's tent, right?"

"I just asked that!" Lucy elbowed Jack, who went sliding off the log the two of them were sharing.

"Hey! I'm dying over here," he cried out. "Have a heart. I can't listen to *everything* you say. I'm only human."

"No, you're only a boy!"

"Why were you at Marcie's tent?" Emily asked. She was now eating a slice of PEI Preserve Company raspberry cheese cake she had been saving.

"As I was saying, I ended up at Marcie's tent for a very good reason." Jack threw the used napkin into the campfire and watched the flames roar up around it. "Since I was in shock, I kinda got lost on my way back and headed in the wrong direction. Before I knew it I was at Marcie's tent. When I realized where I was I quickly turned and started running back to the boys' tent. That's when I tripped over that root and scraped my knee on a rock."

"Goodness Jack! Did Marcie hear you? All we need is for her to be even more suspicious than she already is."

"Lucy! Where's your sympathy for my knee? Who cares about Marcie! What about me? I could have died from exposure out there...or a bear attack. You know, they can smell blood from miles away."

"There're no bears on the island, and exposure is not an issue in the summertime," Lucy snapped. "And I do feel sorry for you, but not because of your knee. There are issues regarding intelligence, and I'm sorry you don't have any!"

"That's cruel!"

"That's life!"

"What about Marcie?" Hannah interrupted.

"She wasn't there." Jack turned to Hannah. "She never came out of the tent. I thought she might be a heavy sleeper, and that's why she didn't hear my crying."

"You were crying?"

"I never said that," Jack coughed. "Anyway, what I was saying was that there were no sounds coming from the tent, so I peeked in through one of the screen windows. She had left one of those glow sticks in there, so I could see pretty well. Sleeping bag, pillow, some books, but no Marcie. Needless to say, I was concerned."

"Yes, it was needless to say," Lucy muttered.

"I wonder what she was up to?" Hannah looked at Lucy. "Maybe she also went to visit the bathroom."

"Not unless she was visiting with a friend," Jack said. "As I was heading back to my tent, I cut through this area of the camp. When I came round the corner of the communications tent, I heard voices coming from the trail leading down to the beach. I followed the voices."

"What did you see?" Emily was now eating some crackers and cheese.

"Nothing. It was too dark. But I heard two people talking. I'm sure one of them was Marcie. The other sounded like a man...very deep voice."

"So what were they talking about?" Lucy asked more urgently.

"Couldn't hear all that well, so hard to say," warned Jack. "The wind and the waves on the water were a bit loud, so I only heard bits and pieces. The word *police* was brought up a lot. Emily's name was mentioned, too. Marcie also sounded upset that nothing of any real value was being dug up. She's definitely after something. When the man mentioned Atlantis, she just laughed. Sorry girls, but she didn't sound like she had much faith in your theory of a lost city. Oh yeah, she also mentioned the word *cave*, and *treasure*, and finally *ghost*."

"Ghost?"

"Treasure?"

"Ooooh, this is getting *scary*," Emily moaned.

Ignoring her sister, Hannah turned to Jack and Lucy. "Do you think Marcie was actually talking to that guy we saw in Cavendish, or was it Charlie?"

"Well—it could have been Charlie," Jack thought about it a bit. "I did lose track of him through the woods, so there was no guarantee that he actually got back to his tent. He could have been meeting with Marcie instead. A definite possibility."

"Poor Charlie," Emily said, opening up a bag of corn chips. "I like him."

"He could be our cold-blooded killer," Jack nodded knowingly.

"But no one died," Emily pointed out.

"Still..."

"Why are we talking about dead people?" Izzy's voice cracked, right behind Jack. He jumped in fright and landed hard behind the log, legs splayed in the air.

The kids explained to Izzy all that happened during the night. The old lady was unusually quiet and looked quite tired, with dark circles under eyes. Her bright flowered straw hat stood out in sharp contrast to her pale face. Jack's news worried her.

"I always knew she was up to something," the old woman muttered. "I don't trust her."

"So what do we do?" Lucy asked.

"You young'uns just keep digging," Izzy nodded. "It'll keep you out of trouble."

"Yeah, and away from them ghosts!" Emily said.

"Speaking of ghosts, we'll be having our weekly bonfire tonight, despite our major setback," Izzy said, trying to lighten the mood. "Maybe it'll get our minds off the disappearing armband. One of the best parts of these evenings is the ghost story. Scares the heebee jeebees out of me, guaranteed! And those marshmallows are simply divine. Just hope the rain holds off. It would put a damper on things!"

Laughing at her own joke, Izzy left the foursome. Hannah worriedly watched her as she slowly made her way to the communications tent. Once Izzy had gone inside, Hannah turned to Lucy.

"Do you think she's okay?"

Lucy shrugged. "We'll keep an eye on her, just in case. Let's get ready for our day.

Chapter 10

Ghosts

The day dragged on at a snail's pace. As Jack said, archaeology was backbreaking work, and discoveries were frequently few and far between. The Greenwich dig was no exception. Although Hannah and her friends made steady progress clearing the earth and exposing a couple of stratigraphic layers at a time, no earth-shattering discoveries were made that day.

Marcie often came to visit their site, curious to see if the kids had found anything of interest. By the time five o'clock rolled around, Hannah was tired of seeing red earth. To everyone's delight, Izzy came on the blow horn and called it a day.

After a quick shower all around, preparations were underway for the bonfire night. Luckily the rain had held off during the day, and everyone kept their fingers crossed that the evening would pass without any more moisture. Wood had been specially trucked to the site, since no one was allowed to touch anything within the national park. These places were highly protected environmental areas. When a branch broke off in the forest, it was left where it fell. Eventually that branch would be recycled back into the ground as compost. It was all part of the natural life cycle that Parks Canada was in charge of protecting.

Supper was not the usual grand affair that the kids were used to. Quick sandwiches were washed down with refreshing lemonade and the kitchen was cleaned up and abandoned in record time. Marcie decided to skip the whole supper business. Hannah had seen her leave camp with a backpack, just after Izzy closed the dig for the day. She wondered what the young archaeologist was up to. Charlie, too, was suspiciously missing.

The bonfire was huge! Long logs were spaced around the outer edges of the fire, well away from the flames and heat of the burning wood. Laughter mixed with music. George, one of the lab techs, had hooked up his stereo to a portable generator and lively fiddle music floated throughout the camp. Hannah and Jack busily roasted marshmallows, while Emily and Lucy skewered hot dogs through specially made roasting sticks.

"Now all we need is a good old fashioned ghost story." Hannah chomped down on her marshmallow. After she inhaled a couple of hot dogs, Emily moved on to marshmallows. As Hannah looked on, Emily fought a losing battle with the sticky white stuff. Strings of melted marshmallow stuck to fingers and hair, not to mention her nose and mouth. Another bath was in order. Hannah sighed.

"We were saving this one for tonight." Izzy clapped to get everyone's attention. "Dr. Williams, would you care to do the honours?"

"Izzy, my dear. No one could tell a scary story better than you. You're the best at being scary!"

"Humph! I don't know if that was a compliment or an insult," Izzy harrumphed. Out of the corner of her eye Hannah noticed that Marcie was back. She kept well away from the group, but obviously tried to listen in on the campfire conversation. Charlie had been back for hours already, but he also had a secretive look on his face. Hannah saw that Izzy was watching Marcie, too. Hannah elbowed Lucy, nodding her head in Marcie's direction. Lucy's right eyebrow rose up a fraction.

Izzy cleared her throat and began the story.

◆ ◆ ◆

There was a legend in this area of a great hunter. His name was Yuma. He was very skilled, having learned to hunt from his father and grandfather before him. He was also the Chief's son, and he thought he was the best hunter in all the land. Yuma was fearless and bold. He took great risks, but brought back enough meat for his people to live very comfortably. No one was ever hungry.

Great hunting skills also brought great wealth as his people offered him many gifts of thanks for providing such an abundance of food. His village worshipped him, thinking his skills must have come from the spirits themselves because they seemed almost inhuman. He could blend in with the wind and the trees and walk as silently as a mouse. He ran as swiftly as a deer and had the strength of a wild boar. Who but a god could do all of this? But it was not wise to treat a human like a god. It went against the laws of nature.

Then the rains came more frequently to the area, accompanied by great winds, thunder, and lightning. Rumours started that Yuma had angered the spirits with his boasting. The village was worried. The boys who used to be Yuma's friends were now jealous of his skills, and got upset when he told them he was the best hunter. Soon, Yuma found he had no friends. Although he was still treated with respect, he was no longer included in everyday village life. He was alone. This made him angry.

His father, Chief Eagle Feather, was not pleased by what he saw. He tried speaking to his son, but Yuma would not listen. He was too proud to hear the ramblings of an old man. And the Chief was also sick. An old broken leg, injured during a past hunting accident, was causing him problems again. During their most recent hunting expedition, Chief Eagle Feather had been attacked by a wild boar, and he had broken his leg again, in the same place as the old injury. It did not heal properly. Weeks after this last injury, the great Chief died. The villagers mourned his death. It was a great loss. Yuma became Chief of the village. But he did not mourn.

The new Chief needed a wife. But Yuma was not impressed by any girl in his village. He wanted someone as amazing as he was. After months of visiting other neighbouring villages, he found his wife. Her name was Alawa, and she was also a great hunter. Her father, the chief of her village, had no sons, and so he always took Alawa with him to hunt. She learned well and became the best in her village. Alawa was beautiful. Her long black hair was intricately braided with hundreds of red beads woven throughout.

Yuma was finally impressed. He told Alawa many stories about his own skill as a hunter, and what a wonderful chief he was in his own village. She fell in love with Yuma's stories, and he took her back to his village as his wife. Her gift to Yuma was a set of matching jewelled armbands. They had been left to Alawa by her father, to be used during her lifetime. But when she died, these armbands would have to be returned to her village. They were gifts from the gods, and they had to come back to their original home, otherwise the spirits would be furious and demand vengeance!

Alawa's village was devastated by her departure. Worse yet, her father was furious. He did not want his daughter marrying Yuma. He didn't like Yuma. When he found out that she had left without his permission, and that she had also taken the armbands, the Chief put a curse on Yuma, asking the spirits for revenge against the man who took his daughter against his wishes.

◆ ◆ ◆

Suddenly thunder boomed off in the distance. Hannah looked up at the sky. No sign of stars. She felt Emily huddling closer.

◆ ◆ ◆

Soon after arriving at Yuma's village, Alawa found that her new husband was not as well-liked as he had led her to believe. In fact, everyone hated him. As a result, she was not made welcome. This was terrible, and Alawa cried every night for the friends and family she had left behind. Then one day she was invited to go hunting with her husband. She thought that if she came back with something she hunted herself, perhaps then the village would accept her. Hours later, Yuma stumbled back into his camp, carrying a bloody bundle of rags in his arms. It was Alawa. She was dead, killed by a wild bear. Stuttering through the telling of the story, Yuma explained how his wife had tried to kill the bear, but the arrow missed its heart. Instead, it landed in the bear's shoulder, and the bear got very angry and charged Alawa, killing her.

But Yuma lied. It was in fact his own arrow that had missed. As the bear charged her husband, Alawa ran to Yuma's rescue. The bear, thinking he was again under attack, turned his anger on Alawa and slashed her across the neck with his long claws.

The village was in an uproar. If only Yuma had

been the one killed by the bear. Even though the villagers hated Alawa, they despised her husband even more.

Poor Alawa. She was mourned by no one. Even Yuma was more upset by the fact that his arrow had missed the bear than by the death of his wife. He went to bed that night wondering about his hunting skill and what could have gone wrong. Could it be the curse put on him by Alawa's father?

Hours after he had finally fallen asleep, Yuma was suddenly awakened. He sat up in his tent, shrugging off the animal hides he used as a blanket. He was alone. But what woke him? He listened closely. The wind howled through the tree. The moans of the leafy giants made eerie and haunting noises. They almost sounded human; like someone in pain, shrieking in the night. The hairs on Yuma's arms suddenly stood up.

What was that? That sound! It was like...

Quickly he jumped and faced the back of the tent. Something was scratching at the sides of the rawhide.

SCCCRRRAAATTTCCCHHH. Slowly. It happened again...

SCCCRRRAAATTTCCCHHH.

Something wanted to come in. Taking the knife from his belt, Yuma slowly backed out of the tent and quietly circled around the back. He could still hear the terrifying scratching sounds tearing at the tent. He rounded the last corner quietly and suddenly jumped out, ready to attack.

No one was there. And yet...the scratching continued.

SSCCCRRRAAATTTCCCHHH.

"Who's there?" he whispered hoarsely.

The scratching stopped.

It had to be an animal, he thought. It had to! What else could it be? He ran back towards his tent. He made it as far as the tent's opening.

"EEEEEEEEEEEEEE!" A high pitched shriek pierced the night wind.

"Who's there?" Yuma cried. "Show yourself!"

But Yuma saw nothing. He jumped inside the tent and closed the flap. Huddled in the middle of the fur hides, Yuma clutched his knees to his chest, trying to stop the shaking.

Scratch! Scraaaatttcchhhh! This time the sound came from the tent flap. And the flap was moving...very, very slowly. It was horrible. Was it just the wind? With his eyes, he followed the scratching. It started at the top of the tent flap, and slowly made its way down.

Ever...so...slowly...

Then it stopped close to the bottom. Again, silence. Then...a small white hand eased its way around the flap and stopped. It was deathly white but covered with splotches of what looked like dried blood. Yuma could still see the rough hide of the tent through that terrible hand. In a flash, the pale nails suddenly dug into the tent, claws gripping the leather hide of the door...pulling... tearing...ripping!

Yuma could hardly breathe. He recognized the hand. It was his wife's. Alawa. She was back! But how can that be? She was dead!

If he had had the courage to grab the hand and pull it further inside, he knew he would see her armband—the armband he never gave back to her people—the match to the one still on his arm! He knew he should have removed that armband when he lit the fire under Alawa's funeral pyre. But he could not touch her. She represented his failure. Instead, he had turned and walked away from her burning body.

"What do you want?" he shouted.

Instead of replying, the hand released the door and reached towards Yuma, as if expecting him to give it something. It moved closer. And closer— until he saw the armband. The brilliant yellow gold

shone fiercely, and the green and red gems sparkled with an unearthly light. "NOOOOOOO!"
he yelled, and angrily slapped at the hand.

But of course there was nothing there.

◆ ◆ ◆

Again, the thunder boomed, and Hannah jumped.
The storm was still far out over the water. Izzy
paused in her story to listen to its approach. With
a shaky sigh, she continued...

◆ ◆ ◆

A new day dawned, bright and sunny.

Yuma the coward was no longer the man he
was before his wife's death. He jumped at the
slightest sound. He yelled at anyone who came
near him. He no longer hunted to feed his village.
And he did not sleep.

For eight nights, he was visited by his dead
wife. Her ghostly hand scratched at the tent,
searching for her precious armband.

Yuma was slowly going insane. And worse
yet, no one believed his story about the nightly
visits.

Finally, on the ninth night, another storm blew
through the village. Shrieks and howls pierced the
wicked night. Yuma swore to anyone who would
listen that he could hear his wife wailing all

through the night. But no one paid any attention to the ranting of a madman.

And the horrible scratching continued.

SSCCCRAAATTTCCCHH...

Yuma couldn't take it anymore. He grabbed the armband and yanked it off his arm and hurled it toward the white claw that had invaded his tent yet again. Without bothering to look, he shrank into a corner of the tent and covered his head with his shaking hands. He screamed and screamed and screamed.

The next morning, Straight Arrow, one of the braver men of the village, went to look in on Yuma. Everyone had heard the terrible screams coming out of Yuma's tent during the night, but no one came to help. They were all too afraid.

Yuma was still huddled against the back of the tent, his face buried in his knees. He was not moving. Straight Arrow saw that Yuma was dead.

As he was removed from the tent, a single red bead fell out of his mouth.

The next day was Yuma's funeral. As the villagers approached the funeral pyre, the same pyre where Alawa had been laid to rest, they found an odd sight. There, amid blackened pieces of wood and rock, lay two golden armbands, sparkling in the summer sun. The villagers picked out the armbands and placed the body of Yuma on the pyre. Straight Arrow struck a flint stone and lit it.

As the flames roared around the body, something in the woods shrieked! A wild animal? Perhaps. The next day, that same brave man who had found Yuma dead in his tent ran to Alawa's village and handed back the armbands.

The shrieking was never heard again.

◆ ◆ ◆

Suddenly a huge explosion shattered the silence, quickly followed by a series of smaller bangs and pops. The sky lit up with multi-coloured flames. Fireworks! Everyone clapped as the mini-bombs exploded above their heads. When it was all done, Charlie stood up and took a bow.

"Well, that's one mystery solved," Lucy whispered in Hannah's ear.

Dr. Williams thanked Charlie for setting up the fireworks that afternoon, without burning off any fingers or blowing up the dig sites. Another hearty round of applause, and everyone took it as a sign to break up and call it a night.

Hannah turned to Izzy and thanked her for the story. "I liked the way you wove in the story of the armbands. Nice touch."

"Actually, that's a story that I heard a while back," Izzy explained. "It's been passed down by the aboriginal people for a few centuries now."

"Do you think that the armband that we found is actually one of the pieces in the story?" Lucy asked.

"Could be! The Mi'kmaq people were already on the island when the Europeans arrived. Other Aboriginal groups inhabited the island before the Mi'kmaqs. And the cultures from one period to another could have mixed, intermarrying and sharing stories. I would guess that this story could have been passed down from one cultural group to another over thousands of years. Who knows when it started?"

Then she heard a whimper...

"What was that?"

Hannah realized that Emily was no longer at her side, pulling on her arm. Instead, she was huddled behind Jack. Her black sweatshirt, Jack's windbreaker *and* Lucy's fleece jacket were all tightly wound around her head. Clutched in between her hands was the unfortunate bag of marshmallows she had used to muffle her screams. She was humming to herself.

With the help of her friends, Hannah managed

to pry the marshmallows from Emily's sticky fingers, while Lucy and Jack unwound the layers of clothes from around her head.

Ghost stories just aren't your thing, Emzo, thought Hannah, as she escorted her shaking sister back to their tent. She hoped the nightmares would not be too loud tonight.

Chapter 11

Defection

The next day Hannah and her friends were back at work. According to Izzy, they had another day or two of digging before they hit pay dirt.

"Didn't Izzy say that the Cavendish armband and marble were found in the Maritime Archaic Age level?" Emily looked towards Hannah. "Way down thousands of feet? I'm tired of digging. I need more direct stimulation."

"Yeah, also known as the Neolithic period, or Stone Age," Hannah nodded. Her corner of the dig site was already over a metre down. "I did some more research on that. There are some good books back in Dr. Williams' tent. You should take a look at them. That might stimulate you."

"You've got to be kidding! That means reading," Emily shook her head. "Why waste my time when I have a walking encyclopedia for a sister.

Sometimes you're very convenient. Most times, however, you annoy me. Much like this shovel is annoying me right now."

"Didn't that period go from about 9000 B.C. to 3500 B.C.?" Jack interrupted before Hannah had time to argue with Emily.

"Yes, it did," Hannah continued. "You finally learned something! But remember, just because we found the armband in that layer doesn't necessarily mean it dates back to 9000 years ago. It could be even older. Imagine that! What I find even more fascinating is that no one has found any other evidence of gold or marble artifacts on the island going that far back. Both those materials don't come from here. Lots and lots of sandstone, but no marble, and certainly no gold."

"So..."

"So, I think both those artifacts were made by a culture that was very ahead of its time, like Atlantis," Hannah said excitedly, brushing dirt from her knees. "For some reason they paid a visit to this island and brought some of their treasures with them. Why did they come, and what happened to them is a mystery. I think something terrible drove them away from their original home. Now we have to figure out why they disappeared. Isn't archaeology amazing?

So many mysteries to solve! We're the ultimate detectives!"

The storm they heard last evening as they listened to the ghost story had finally made it to the island. Within minutes after the first rumble of thunder, it started raining. Everyone scrambled to quickly cover their pits with blue plastic tarps.

"Let's go see what they're up to in the comm tent," Jack shouted as he glanced behind him to make sure the girls were following. He had his multi-pocket safari jacket over his head, but it was raining so hard that the jacket was soaked within minutes.

"Stop flicking mud on my t-shirt," Lucy cried.

"Stop following so close on my heels," Jack yelled back.

"You're too slow." Lucy gracefully jumped over a puddle.

"Eat my dirt!" Jack laughed and took off at a fast sprint.

Oh boy, Hannah thought. Big mistake! Just a couple of feet ahead lay a massive puddle into which Jack plunged with deadly good aim.

The girls pulled up short beside the reddish brown puddle.

"Oh, lordy!" Emily mumbled.

"Way too cool," Lucy clapped.

"Brilliant!" Hannah shook her head in disbelief.

Small waves still rippled on the surface of the puddle, deformed a bit by splotches of rain that continued to fall. Jack lay smack dab in the middle. Or at least they thought it was him. It was kind of hard to tell. Visibility was not one hundred percent. But still...they could just make out a human shape underneath all that mud. Sort of...

"Well...is anyone going to help me up?" Jack gurgled as he lifted his head above the water, his safari jacket still draped over his back. He must have tried to stop the fall with his arms, because they splayed straight out from his body and stuck down into the mud.

"Come on. I'm being sucked in. This stuff's like quicksand."

Lucy looked back at Hannah, and Hannah looked back at Emily. Emily looked back and found no one else to look at. So Emily took off.

Hannah sighed. So much for that.

"Lucy, you take the left arm, and I'll yank him up from the right. And we have to pull hard. That mud looks like it's got a huge hold on him."

"Really Hannah, can't we just leave him here?"

After taking a minute or so to think it

through, Hannah shook her head and sighed. "Unfortunately not. Someone's sure to find him, and then he'll come after us. It's safer to help him. Besides, we might need him in the future. You know, to help with the digging and all."

"Ladies," *spit, gurgle, burp,* "I'm still here! Just get me out, will you?"

Another sigh.

"On the count of three...one...two...THREE! Pull!"

"With a great sucking sound, the muddy red puddle reluctantly released Jack.

Hannah was trying really hard not to laugh. "Why on earth couldn't you just run through the puddle?"

"I thought about that for a second or so, but then that would have been too simple, no? Listen Sherlock. That puddle hid a very deep and very big hole. And I found it. See, Jack-Jack, the great discoverer, finds an amazing and ancient armband, perhaps even from Atlantis, and then has the good fortune of discovering this super-duper incredible hole. I'm going for a shower. I'm feeling mud oozing into cracks that should never see mud."

"Ewwww, gross!" Lucy gagged.

"Tell me about it," Jack groaned as he limped off stiff-legged to the temporary showers set up on the far side of the camp.

Once everyone was gathered for lunch, Hannah noticed that Izzy was absent. "Has anyone seen her today? I'm a bit worried about her. She didn't look her best yesterday. And did you notice, she was not swearing as much either."

"But she told a really scary story," Emily gulped, swallowing a large mouthful of chicken and rice.

The rain kept up all afternoon. Some of the crew came and invited the kids to a board game in the comm tent. Someone else brought movies, and *Harry Potter and the Prisoner of Azkaban* played at 2:00 p.m. Still no signs of Izzy.

Hannah finally caught a glimpse of Izzy when the group gathered for supper. It was sandwiches again. Izzy joined them just as Hannah was picking out the tomato and lettuce from her chicken sandwich.

"How ya doin' kids?" she asked. "And why you takin' out all them good things from that sandwich of yours, Hannah girl?"

"Hannah doesn't eat real food," Emily chimed in. "She survives on junk."

"Emily!" Hannah shot her sister a warning look.

"Whew! What lousy screwy weather. Can't believe it's still raining. Damn site will be a mud bath. Did you kids cover up your square? Ahhhhh, what's the use anyway? Got some bad news today. Police called. Went down to talk to one of 'em this afternoon. The lab got back with the results of the security tape. There was no fiddling with it. Tape's clean. The armband had to have gone on its disappearin' act before getting to the university. Damned shame. So it looks like a friggin' inside job. We've got an undesirable on the loose. What's that expression? Lion among the bunnies?"

"Isn't it more like, the fox is loose in the chicken coop?" Lucy suggested.

"Guess that's close enough of an example of what I meant," Izzy snorted. She still looked pale and tired, but her insults were back.

"Hey, Jacko! What'd you do to your skin? Give yourself a facial, or what? It's all red! Ooohh, but soooo smooth, like a baby's round little butt. What's your secret, honey buns?"

"A mud bath," Jack mumbled under his breath, swatting away Izzy's hand as she tried to stroke his cheek again.

"A what? I'm a bit hard of hearing, so you gotta speak up, lovey."

"He fell down splat! Right in the middle of a mud puddle," Emily laughed.

"It was more like a crater, not a puddle," Jack corrected. "And that news of yours about the theft of the armband being an inside job is not very comforting for those of us who sleep here among the criminal element. Personally, I think our man is Charlie. He's been so nervous about things lately that he can't sleep. That's why he has to go to the bathroom every half hour. I get like that too when I have to take a math test. I hate math. Too many numbers."

"Okay! Let's get back to the subject at hand. Who stole the armband and why?" Lucy nudged Hannah. "Let's see your notes."

Hannah bent down and picked up her backpack lying at her feet. Flipping over the top flap, she rummaged around a bit and came out with some chocolate bars, a half-eaten bag of chips, and finally her dog-eared yellow notebook. She read off her list.

Missing: *golden armband with jewels.*
Design: *Snake head and tail. Approximate visual dating from the Maritime Archaic Age, about 9000 years old, according to expert Izzy.*

Question: *from Atlantis time period? Striking similarities with other artifacts from the Age of Atlantis.*

Problem: *far away from geographic zone of Atlantis (Mediterranean).*

Opportunity: *The armband could only have been stolen*

a) from the truck while still at the Cavendish site (therefore it could have been anyone who worked at the dig and stayed behind),

or b) before it was carried into the university vault where cameras recorded everything,

or c) after Marcie and Charlie left the university, in which case someone tampered with the videotape from the security camera.

Suspects:

1) Marcie Sullivan, archaeologist. Last person to handle the armband. In charge of depositing it in the university's vault. Said she put the case holding the armband on top shelf at university. Lied about meeting a man after everyone had left the Cavendish dig.

2) Charlie, student. Stayed with Marcie, and drove the armband back to university. Said he always stayed in the truck, and the armband never left his sight. Also said he saw no one at

*the dig site talking to Marcie. Could they be in it
together?*

*3) Dr. Williams, dig foreman. This is his last
dig, and he wants to retire in style and make it
big. He was one of the last to see the armband
before it was placed in the box and sealed.*

"Might as well put me on your list of suspects
too," Izzy sighed. "After all, I was the last one
to wrap up the armband and place it in its safe
container. Dr. Williams was my witness. We could
potentially be in on it together, and never have
really put the armband into the case."

"But you can't be the thief," Emily yelped.
"You're too old!"

"Thanks for the compliment," laughed Izzy.
"But I could be one of those frustrated archaeologists desperately seeking that elusive discovery
of a lifetime—and then when I finally find it, I
want it all to myself so that I can become famous,
and write papers on it, and have it in my own
private collection."

"Wow!"

"Not really, but I had fun saying that!" Izzy
stood up.

"I think we should put that mysterious man
down on our list." Lucy looked at Hannah. "You

know, the guy she met with after everyone left the Cavendish dig."

Hannah nodded and wrote it down as point 4.

"I still think that guy was just some stupid lost tourist who stumbled on the dig site, like I told you when we met the coppers," Izzy grumbled. "But if it makes you happy, put him on your list. It looks more professional."

With Izzy's encouragement, Hannah also added Izzy's name to the list.

"Personally, I think Charlie sticks out like a sore thumb." Jack looked up at Izzy. "He has motive, because he's probably poor and needs the money. All his clothes have holes in them. Remember, clothes make the man! So he decides to sell the armband on the black market to afford some decent Calvin Klein jeans. If he was telling the truth about staying in the truck all that time, how could the armband disappear? It doesn't make sense, unless he was in on it."

"And I think its Marcie, because she lied about her boyfriend," Lucy added. "Anyone who lies about a boy has serious issues."

"We need to talk to Charlie ASAP!" Hannah closed her notebook with a snap. "Jack, you followed him a couple of nights ago. You told us that he disappeared at some point during the night. He could have been meeting with Marcie, since she was gone too. Was she meeting Charlie, or her boyfriend? We've already tried talking to Marcie, but she denies even having a boyfriend, so that's no good. Let's try our luck with Charlie."

"You'll have to wait a bit on that," Izzy advised as she started walking away. "Charlie Bones is back at the university conducting some soil sample tests. In fact, they came from your pit. We might have some interesting results on the age of your little square out there. He should be back tomorrow morning to report on the lab results."

The next morning the world turned upside down. The rain continued to fall and small lakes of reddish-brown mud flooded paths and pits. Hannah heard generators chugging away, pumping out water from some of the deeper pits, in an effort to keep up with the falling rain. Both students and professors were running around laying down wood planks on the main pathways leading to the comm and dining tents. Other people had also fallen in the mud, and Dr. Williams wanted to prevent more messy accidents.

As Hannah neared the dining tent, she saw

Jack running from the direction of the men's sleeping units. Wide-eyed, he pulled up short, panting from the run. "The police are here! They just arrested Charlie. They think he did it."

"But what about Marcie? She could have easily done it, too!" Hannah gasped.

Just then Izzy shuffled over, a bright pink and lime-green polka dot umbrella held high above her head. "Let's get out of this hellish rain and reassess this in private, shall we?"

Fifteen minutes later, Izzy managed to round up Emily and Lucy, and all four kids were sitting in Izzy's tent, huddled around her portable propane heater. Being one of the lead managers of this dig certainly had privileges, Hannah thought. It was comfy and warm in the tent, and everyone was enjoying a nice cup of hot chocolate and homemade fudge.

"Dear old Marcie is a stooge," Izzy said, struggling to light her pipe. She lifted the fifth match to the bowl of tobacco and everyone waited with bated breaths to see if she would finally succeed. "Damned wet weather! Can't an old woman enjoy a decent smoke once in a while? Too damp out here for these ancient bones of mine, but it seems this tobacky ain't likin' it much either. Oh well, guess I'll have to find another sin. Jacko, got any chewing tobacky?"

"Do you mean chewing *tobacco*? The stuff that gives you mouth *cancer*?"

"That'll be the one."

"Nope. Just ran out."

"Frig!"

"Why did they arrest Charlie, and not Marcie?" Hannah interrupted, frowning at Jack. "I mean, she could be just as guilty."

"And she had a good motive for taking the armband...like fame," Lucy cut in. "Finding a lost civilization here on the island would really make her career. She wouldn't have to worry about getting research grants at all. The money would be rolling in, and she would be a hero in the archaeological community."

"Well, our dear little Marcie rolled on poor Charlie Bones." Izzy continued to rummage through the rest of her tote bags. "She finally admitted to the police that she had taken a half hour break with her boyfriend, while Charlie waited for her in the truck. That gave Charlie lots of time to be alone with the armband and crack the safe. Marcie said he probably buried it somewhere in Cavendish and went back for it later that evening. She told the cops that when she went back to the truck, he was gone. She shouted for him a couple of times until he finally came out of the bushes in front of the truck. Marcie told the police that when she saw him, he looked very guilty."

"What was her excuse for lying to us about *the boyfriend*?" Emily pretended to stick her finger down her throat and gag.

"She didn't want to tell anyone about him, because we would all tease her. Damn right we would, but that's beside the bloody point. Oh yeah, she also mentioned that he was a very shy in-di-vi-du-al! My arse! What a load of crap! Excuse my French. Need to calm down, old girl. Take a deep breath. All this frustration is not good for you."

"You okay, Miss Izzy?" Lucy placed a warm hand on the old woman's knee.

"Yes, yes," Izzy gently patted Lucy's hand. "I'm just a tad bit upset. This was supposed to be my last dig, and I wanted it to be spectacular. But this kind of spectacular was not what I had in mind, know what I mean? It's all a huge and disappointing mess!"

"Not to mention muddy."

Izzy told the kids how Marcie insisted she never checked on the box before it left Cavendish, taking it for granted that it was all nicely tucked away in the safe. And of course the safe had both her and Charlie's fingerprints all over it, since they both opened and closed it. According to the police Marcie's fingerprints were the most prominent on the safe's handle, but as she explained, she was the last one who opened the safe back at the university, so hers *would* be the ones on top."

"It sounds like she has an explanation for everything," Jack said, shaking his head. "Well, so much for talking to Charlie now. How did you find out all this info, Miss Izzy?"

"I was there when Marcie spoke to the coppers," Izzy explained. "She called them here this morning to confess. She wanted me to stick around and act like a witness to the whole thing. I think the young hussy just wanted me to spread the word to everyone here at camp about what she said."

"Great," Lucy sighed. "Now I really don't know who to believe."

"We'll let the police figure this out," Izzy said, gently patting Lucy on the knee. "In the meantime, Paul, the communications guy, will be taking the four of you to town for some fun and games. Unless you're a lab tech, you can't do much in this rain, so why waste a day of your summer vacation."

Chapter 12

Dunking and Spelunking!

"IZZY'S HAD A HEART ATTACK!"

Jack crashed into the tent where the girls were just putting the finishing touches on their outfits. Doubled over and panting from his sprint across the camp, Jack fought to catch his breath before continuing. "I just met Dr. Williams. He was heading over to the comm tent to tell everyone."

"When did all this happen?" Hannah grabbed Jack by the collar of his multi-coloured Hawaiian shirt. "Where did they take her? How did this happen? Is Izzy alright? Can we go see her? What do we do now? Was it the stress of everything that's happening here? How are we going to solve this mystery without her?"

Jack leaned forward and kissed Hannah smack dab on the mouth!

Hannah was shocked again, but this time into silence.

"There, that worked like a charm," he smiled.

"OUFF!" Jack bent over again, this time furiously rubbing his shin. A well aimed kick from Hannah was her wordless reply to his attempt at romance.

Within minutes, the whole camp was gathered in the dining tent, waiting for Dr. Williams to fill them in on the latest news to hit this seemingly cursed dig.

"Can I have everyone's attention, please," Dr. Williams began. He cleared his throat and waited for folks to settle down. "As you've probably all heard by now, our dear Miss Izzy has suffered a slight setback. Indeed, she did have a small heart attack—now, now, let's not panic..." he warned. He fought to speak over the sudden eruption of noise.

"SHE'S OKAY!" He had to shout.

"I just came from the Queen Elizabeth Hospital in Charlottetown," he went on. "Izzy's doctor told me it was a very mild attack, almost like a warning, really. They unblocked one of the arteries leading to her heart. Minor surgery, and now she's on some blood thinning medications. That being said, she's a bit tired, but in very good spirits. She can't wait to come back to the dig and find that elusive Atlantis!—and that's what we should be doing in her honour. So let's go play in some dirt!"

A noticeable sigh of relief rippled through the crowd, and a few minutes later everyone was hungrily digging in to their breakfasts of pancakes and sausages. Talk was still subdued, but the atmosphere was a lot more positive than it had been before the impromptu meeting.

"I guess that explains a lot." Hannah looked thoughtful. She was concentrating hard as she poured litres of syrup on a single pancake. "I thought Izzy was looking a bit pale and tired these last few days. I knew the theft of the armband was bothering her, but I guess it was a bit more than that."

"Yeah, looks like it." Jack heaped his plate with a pyramid of sausages and about six pancakes. "Everyone's been upset with what's been happening here, you know, what with Charlie being arrested, and Marcie acting all funny. Speaking of which, where is our lovesick traitor, anyway?"

After looking around the tent, the kids noted that Marcie was suspiciously absent. "Maybe she's visiting Izzy in the hospital," Lucy suggested.

"Or she's with her *boy*friend." Emily made kissy-kissy noises. "Let's go check her tent. Maybe she slept in!"

"Hold your horses!" Jack warned. He speared a juicy piece of sausage with his fork. "First things first! We need to take care of our personal engines and stoke them with some fuel."

"Stuff it, Jack! You're just so full of it!" Lucy rolled her eyes. "...but you're right. We'll eat first, and then go check."

Thirty minutes later the foursome stood in front of Marcie's tent, shuffling their feet uncertainly.

"Who's going to knock?" Hannah whispered.

"Not me!" Lucy hissed.

Jack stuffed his hands in his pants pockets and began to whistle tunelessly under his breath.

"You guys are such babies," Emily snapped. She stomped over to the tent's zippered door and hit the flap with the palm of her hand. "Wakey, wakey! Marcie? Rise and shine, sunshine. It's time to do some digging and get scientifical!"

"Scientifical? What on earth does that mean?" Hannah frowned at her sister.

"We're working on science stuff, and so we're being scientifical," the Emzo explained very slowly, making sure Hannah understood. "I can't believe that Miss Bookworm here doesn't know that word. Just goes to show, I'm not as dumb as you think I am."

Hannah and Lucy just stared at Emily, not sure what to say next. All this time however, Marcie's tent remained quiet.

"Hmm." Jack tapped a finger on his lips. "Maybe she *is* at the hospital. Emily, take a peek inside the tent."

Emily freed the tent's zipper from the mud on the ground and slowly zipped the door a quarter of the way up. Still on her knees, she squeezed her head through the small opening and looked inside. She waited a few seconds for her eyes to adjust to the sudden darkness, and then was able to make out a pillow and sleeping bag, both of which were neatly folded. There was nothing else, including Marcie, in the tent.

Emily pulled her head back out and was about to let the others know that Marcie was gone when she suddenly stiffened. "Hannah? Hannah? HANNAH! OWWWW! Help me!"

All three kids dropped to their knees next to Emily. Hannah put her hand on her sister's back. "What's wrong, Emzo?"

"It's awful, and it hurts whenever I move!" she wailed.

"What's awful?" Jack wailed back.

"My hair!" Emily cried.

"We know your hair is awful," Hannah shrugged. "It always is! So what?"

"Listen, fart face, my hair is stuck in the zipper!" Emily yelled. "I can't move! Get it undone! NOOWW!"

"Wait...this is our chance—let's leave her here." Hannah quickly stood up.

"Ha ha! Funny! Now get me out of here. And no scissors, got it?"

With a little bit of work, Hannah freed all but a few short blond hairs.

Everyone got back to work, although still a bit preoccupied with thoughts of Izzy and Marcie. As the hours dragged by, Marcie still had not come back to camp. By the end of the day, Hannah was extremely suspicious. Was it coincidence that the day after Charlie was arrested, and Izzy had her heart attack, Marcie just upped and disappeared? Even Dr. Williams was worried. He had that scrunched up look on his face that grown-ups get when they're not happy. What was going on?

Hannah met up with Jack and Lucy who had just come back from the beach with more bad news.

"The police were here again talking to Dr. Williams," Jack said. "The armband is still missing, and Charlie's not talking. They wanted to question Marcie, but no one knew where she was. Dr. Williams suggested the hospital, but when the police checked with Izzy, they were told that Marcie never showed up. So there goes that theory. Where on earth could she be?"

"Isn't it obvious?" Emily asked. "She knows the heat is on and probably took off with the armband."

"But Charlie's the one that was arrested for stealing it!" Hannah shook her head. "This makes it look like Marcie was in on it too. After all, she's the one who tattled on Charlie. Was it to get him out of the way? And now she's gone. With Izzy out of commission, and the dig project falling apart, she probably took off."

"There've been a lot of defections lately. I don't know about you, but I'm beat just thinking about it!" Hannah plopped herself down on a chair as far from Jack as she could get. She still hadn't forgiven him for the kiss and was figuring out interesting ways to torture him. She'd have to google a few ideas.

"Yup, yup." Jack agreed, looking to drag a camp chair closer to Hannah. "Let's go get some grub. We need to keep up our strength for tomorrow."

"What's going on tomorrow?" Lucy asked,

looking at Hannah, who shrugged.

"Lucy, girl! Tomorrow is another day!" Jack laughed.

Groans and moans. Jack's lame jokes, however, no matter how corny, did manage to lift their spirits, and they raced to the kitchen tent. Last one there was a rotten egg!

In the morning the team received another report on Izzy's condition. According to Dr. Williams, the rambunctious archaeologist was itching to get out of bed, and the nurses were having a hard time keeping her confined, He said that Izzy kept throwing her flowered straw hat at any nurse or doctor who tried to take away the cigars she had hidden in her purse. She didn't understand why she wasn't allowed to at least chew on the yummy things. Hannah laughed at that, certain that the old woman's swearing would quickly wear down the medical staff.

During breakfast many of the team members decided to carpool and visit Izzy in the hospital. "I think they really want to see the chaos Izzy's causing at the hospital," Jack chuckled. "It must be quite a show. Sounds like everyone's going."

"Everyone but us! Too bad kids can't go visit," Emily moped.

"Hospital policy for heart patients," Lucy sniffed. "Guess they don't want people getting too excited, and kids tend to do that to adults."

"I don't see how that's possible," Emily shrugged, slouching over a mug of hot chocolate.

When she looked up, a white spot of whipped cream was stuck to the tip of her nose. Emily didn't feel it. "I know for a fact that we can be quite calm and soothing influences. Just like dogs. Did you know they use dogs for pet therapies, bringing them to hospitals to visit patients? I would think that kids would be just as good therapy as dogs. If dogs can jump on beds, so can kids. And we can bounce higher than dogs. That would make for an even better show for the patients, don't you agree? And did any of you notice that Marcie's still not back? I think you were right! She's on the lam. Fugitive on the run with an ancient armband. *Burp!* Oops, sorry. That hot chocolate was delicious, especially the second time up. I'm going to get some more."

Hannah, Jack, and Lucy watched Emily skip off towards the chef.

"Is anyone going to tell her about the you-know-what?" Jack asked, pointing to his nose.

"Why bother," Hannah shrugged. "Knowing Emily, she'd probably leave it on."

An hour later the camp was almost empty. Most of the crew was on their way to Charlottetown to visit Izzy. Emily decided to go for a walk along the beach and look for sea shells and driftwood for future arts and crafts projects. Jack and Lucy sat down to a game of chess at some tables near the campfire. Hannah thought of joining them, but instead she decided to write in her notebook.

All of a sudden, Emily came dashing through the woods and zoomed past the kitchen tent, stumbling into some of the empty camp chairs around the fire.

"Guess who I saw?" she gasped, trying to detangle herself from the chairs. "Marcie's boyfriend! I was doing my cartwheels on the beach when I fell in the water, which just happened to be full of sea grass. Did I tell you I fell head first into the ocean? Well, I did, and the stupid stinky grass went all over my hair! I need to wash it. *Anyways*! While I was sitting in the sand, I heard someone laugh and thought it was you, Hannah. I was about to yell at you, dear sister, when I saw it was Marcie's boyfriend. He was just up on one of those rocky ridges. Tall, dark hair, wearing a baseball cap. Still couldn't make out his face, because he was a bit too far from me. But I know it was him."

"Where'd he go?"

"Did you follow him?"

"Of course I followed him," Emily snorted as she pulled the fifth piece of seaweed from her braids. "I saw him heading off in the direction of Marcie's tent, so I ran after him..."

"And?!"

"And I lost him," Emily finished.

"That's just fluffing bad luck!" Jack moaned.

"Watch your language," Lucy snapped.

"I said fluffing..." said Jack.

"The meaning is still clear, and we know what you would've liked to say!" Hannah added.

Turning back to the others, she said "We need to tell someone that the boyfriend was here. We need to call the police. If they catch this guy, then maybe he could lead them to Marcie."

The kids ran back to the kitchen tent and tried talking to Chef Armando. Armando, up to his elbows in pizza dough and flour, shrugged his shoulders. "Probably some tourist who got lost. Greenwich is a National Park, you know, and tourists run around here all day."

"But they're not allowed around the dig site. The area is blocked off with 'No Trespassing' signs everywhere," Hannah said irritably.

"Besides, we know who it is," Emily added.

"He's Marcie's boyfriend!"

Armando laughed hysterically. "You've got to be kidding! Marcie has a boyfriend? I've never even seen her look at a man. Why don't you kids go play in the sand? Make some nice castles or something. Goodness knows we have enough shovels around here that you could use. Run along now and let me work on my creation."

"But—"

"Tsk, tsk, tsk. No buts," Armando said, waving a white finger in the air. "Vamoose before I spoil my dough. Do you want to take the blame if supper gets ruined?"

As the kids reluctantly shuffled out of the kitchen tent, Jack scratched his head. "We've just been dismissed. Why do kids have such a hard time convincing adults about important things?"

"Such as?

"Such as a major crime being committed right under their nose? I always thought that was just an exaggeration you found in books and movies. Who would have thought that really happened? Not me! Everyone always listens to me."

"Listen yes, believe no!" When they got back to their tent, Hannah threw down her notebook beside her chair.

"What do we do now?" Jack slumped into

Hannah's chair, oblivious of Hannah's dirty look.

"Whatcha folks up to?" Wayne Simpson, Hannah's neighbour, poked his head into the tent and then sat down heavily in the chair next to Jack. "Lookit you lazing round on such a gorgeous sunshiny day! You modern things don't know what to do with yerselves if you ain't got all your electronic gizmos wrapped around your itty bitty chicken fingers."

Reaching into the front pocket of a frayed blue jean shirt, Wayne pulled out a square package. "Care for a smoke?"

"We don't smoke, sir." Jack frowned.

"I know that, little dingbat! But do you want to try some of this?" Wayne waved the package in front of Jack's face.

Lucy, who was the only one who knew what was going on, shook her head. "That joke's getting old, Mr. Wayne," she said.

"Ain't old when some green horn's still falling for it, right?" he cackled as he slapped Jack on the back.

"Ouch!"

Lucy sighed and explained what was what. "Mr. Wayne quit smoking last year, and he replaced his bad habit with a better habit: chewing gum. He just offered you some Juicy Fruit, Jack."

"Oh, sorry, but no thanks, I'm good, sir." Slowly, Jack picked up his chair and inched away from Wayne. His back was still smarting. "No offense, sir, but why are you here?"

"None taken, poophead," Wayne said, stuffing a couple of pieces of gum in his mouth. "Got a call from Mackenzie, who in turn got a call from Dr. Williams. Seems everyone was concerned about leaving you brats alone today. What with crime being so high here on the island...I was asked to come and keep you comp'ny. So, here I am!"

"Great," Jack mumbled, just out of earshot.

"So, where's our little Frankenstein?" Wayne asked, looking around the campfire. "I don't see no bruised face among you lot..."

Wayne was right, thought Hannah, suddenly aware of the quiet that had followed them out of the kitchen tent. The last time she had seen her sister was when they were trying to convince Armando to call the police. "I don't know where she went. I hate it when she takes off like this without telling me where she's going. With Emily that usually means trouble."

Lucy quickly let Wayne in on the events of the last few days. "We think that one of the suspects in this mystery is right here with us. Unfortunately, no one's here to help us, and the only adult in charge is Armando, the chef—"

"Who was no help at all," Jack added.

"Well, well, well." Wayne yawned loudly, scratching at the two-day growth of stubble on his face. "First order of business is finding my Frankenstein. Can't be hard to miss, what with all them rainbow colours on her face."

"Actually sir, the bruises have faded quite a bit," Jack explained. "Emily looks quite normal, except for the big scab above her eye."

"Oh! Okay. Seems Mighty Mouse heals fast. Then it's back to calling her Fidget the Midget, I guess." Wayne stood up. "Let's start the search."

"Why are we always looking for Emily?" Hannah complained as she scooped up her notebook from the ground. "I bet she went looking for Marcie's boyfriend."

"Then she'll be easy to find." Wayne looked around at the gang of friends and thought hard. "Lucy girl, you have the honour of searching with big ole me. *We'll* look round these nice cool woods. Hannah, you take that young whippersnapper Jacko by the hand and explore the beach area, where it's now hot and sunny. Mind, don't go in the water. Current's strong today."

With a wink at Hannah, Wayne grabbed Lucy's hand and dragged her towards the path leading through the woods, whistling a tune in between shouts of "FRANKENSTEIN!" and "Where are you my little midget?"

Lucy turned to Hannah and silently mouthed the word, *help!*

Hannah shrugged helplessly. *Sorry*, she mouthed back.

Considering the circumstances with Wayne being here, Hannah couldn't blame Emily for staying hidden. Lucy glanced back at Hannah and Jack, with a desperate look on her face. While Hannah threw her hands up in frustration, Jack merrily waved to the departing duo. *Oops!* Hannah though, *that was bad luck*. Lucy had caught Jack's wave and grin. Jack was going to pay for that.

When Lucy and Wayne disappeared around a particularly large elm, Jack and Hannah made their way down the beach path. Before starting, Jack had to run back to his tent. He insisted on filling up his pink backpack with all sorts of essentials: Flashlight, rope, Swiss Army knife, chocolate bars, cookies, chips, candy, an apple, matches, tissues, and loads more.

"What do you need all that stuff for?" Hannah watched Jack stuffing the last of the items into backpack. It was near to bursting. "And who's going to carry that junk when your back gives out?"

"Hannah, my dear, I am a *man*! Have no worries and put your faith in me, your hero. *Ouff!* I'm okay! Just a bit heavy, but I'll be fine."

"Whatever." Hannah watched Jack stumble ahead of her, slightly bent over from the great weight. He turned around abruptly.

"Give me your hand," he demanded.

"No!"

"But Mr. Wayne said I have to hold your hand."

"Shut up and turn around!"

A few minutes later, Jack and Hannah were out in the open, staring at the gentle waves of the gulf washing over the red sand. A thick band of sea grass lined the beach, pushed ashore by the high tide. Hannah knew from experience that the seaweed would be gone with the tide change. In the meantime, however, it gave off a mingled smell of fish and salt. She loved it!

The sun was indeed hot, as Wayne had said. Its dazzling rays sparkled off the sea. A gentle breeze helped freshen up the air, but as Hannah and Jack struggled along the sandy beach, the going seemed to get harder and hotter. Cormorants and white terns flew around them, eager to see if the kids had any food to offer. With no sign of a snack, the noisy birds glided towards the line of seaweed. Crabs and other sea life often got trapped in the washed up grass, and the sea birds feasted on the juicy morsels.

They made their way away from the water and climbed the rocky ridge that bordered the beach.

"I need to...adjust my...backpack," Jack whispered hoarsely, dumping the heavy bag on the rocky outcropping. This was where Emily last saw Marcie's boyfriend. Maybe she had come back to have a closer look. So far, however, Jack and Hannah saw no signs of her.

Taking advantage of the break, Hannah grabbed Jack's offensive pink bag and started rifling through it.

"Ah ha! Snack time. Want one?" she asked, waving a Mars bar in front of Jack's face.

"No thanks," he said as he leaned back against the rough cliff wall and closed his eyes. "Just hand me my water bottle, will you? Please?"

Hannah paused.

"...no water bottle, sorry," Hannah said, looking up from the open bag. "Did you pack it? I don't see it."

"It's got to be in there. Look again."

"Nope."

"Nope? Nope what? Nope, it's not in there, or nope, you're not going to look again."

"Both!"

"Oh, give me the bag!"

"Argh!" he groaned. "It must still be in the tent. Can't believe I brought everything else, except a water bottle!"

"No biggie," Hannah laughed. "We won't be out here too long before we need to head back. Emily is probably already at the camp. Look, we'll take out your sleeping bag, and voila, the bag is already much lighter. You don't need this thing to look for Emily anyway."

"We can't just leave it here," Jack yelped, grabbing hold of the sleeping bag and giving it a great big hug.

"We won't," Hannah said, prying Jack's fingers off the shiny blue cover. "No matter how far we go, we still have to make our way back towards this ridge. It's a lot easier walking this way instead of going through the woods. We'll pick up your bag when we're ready to head home."

Reluctantly, Jack heaved himself up. Hannah picked up the backpack and helped Jack pull his arms through the padded straps. Minutes later, they came upon another flat slab of rock sticking out from the cliff face. Large boulders that had crumbled from the main cliff now lay at the bottom of the rock. Deep reds and browns blended in with bright swatches of green along the rock face. A small spring trickled down from the top of the cliff and clinging vines of ivy grew in these pockets of rich dampness.

"I bet that water is delicious," Jack moaned as he gazed up longingly at the clear trickle splashing on the rock above his face. "I'm going to try and get a drink." He shrugged off the heavy pack, reached up above him and firmly grasped the rock. Finding a natural foothold, Jack pulled himself up, directly above the ledge where Hannah stood.

"I'm not sure I'd be drinking that." Hannah told him, squinting against the glare of the sun. The cliff was actually kinda cool, she thought, looking around her. Unlike the sandy ridges closer to the Greenwich dune system, these rocky outcroppings were rough and sharp, with very little sand covering. Deformed by constant wind, crooked pines and birches bent their interesting forms over the edges of the cliffs. They cast a refreshingly cool shade across Hannah's upturned face.

"Hannah, this is soooo cold," Jack yelled down. "You should try it. It's a bit gritty, but thirst-quenching. Come on up. I'll help pull you."

"Strong he-man that you are," Hannah mumbled. Nonetheless, she grabbed Jack's pack and pulled it over her shoulders. Finding the same footholds that Jack had used, Hannah reached up above her, only to find Jack's hand wrapped around her wrist. Without warning, she was yanked up high in the air, landing none too gently beside Jack.

"Isn't this great?" he beamed. "And look what I found over here. See these notches in the rock? It looks like footholds. They're a bit worn away, but it looks like they were man-made. They're too regular to be natural. And if they were made by someone, then that means they should lead to an interesting place. Let's check it out, okay?"

"I don't know," said Hannah slowly, rubbing her wrist. "It looks pretty steep to me. And shouldn't we be looking for Emily?"

"She's probably back at the camp already, just like you said," Jack said, waving his hand towards the far-off dig site. "We'll probably have a great view from up there. Can't miss that, can we?"

Although Hannah was the cautious type, she was also very curious. And it was hard to resist Jack's begging.

"Oh, all right," she finally gave in. "Do you want to bring your pack, or leave it here?"

"I'll get rid of a bit more stuff, so that it's not as heavy."

Out came a small pillow, sun tan lotion and a wind-up radio.

"Never know when you'll need some entertainment, right?"

"You're weird, Jack."

"But you love me."

"Shut up!"

"Okay."

With the pink pack firmly centered on his back again, Jack started up the cliff face, grabbing at anything that looked remotely like it would not break off in his hands. Hannah followed him, stepping exactly in the same spots as Jack. The climb was slow and painful. Hannah bumped her knees several times against roots and stones. Showers of red dirt rained down on her face a couple of times as Jack missed his handholds.

After much grunting and groaning and sweating and swearing, Hannah and Jack finally reached the top of the cliff. Turning, they gazed out to sea.

"Wow, this is amazing Jack," Hannah panted, still breathing hard from the climb. "You can see forever."

"And look down there," he said, pointing towards the beach to his left. "You can see some of the tents from our camp. They look like kites from up here."

"We've certainly come a long way without even realizing it." Hannah was surprised by how high up they were. "I guess we were slowly rising when we walked along the beach. We never noticed we were going uphill."

Turning away from the camp and the sea, Hannah looked around her. They were standing on a small plateau. Low growing blackberry bushes covered the area. Hannah turned to face the pines and birch trees she had noticed before when she was at the bottom of the cliff. These were joined by other trees; beech, ash, and elms towered above her. Just ahead was another cliff, but much smaller than what they had just climbed. It looked oddly triangular. Almost like a perfect shape. Jack was already making his way towards it.

"Ouff!"

Jack suddenly disappeared among the blackberry bushes. Hannah ran to the place where she had seen him just moments ago.

"Are you there?" she asked.

"Yeah! But can you move your foot? You're stepping on my ankle."

"Sorry 'bout that."

"S'alright," he mumbled, trying to pull himself free of the thorny blackberry bushes. "There's a hole here. Let's bend some of these bushes back and see what's under here."

Using their feet to stomp the prickly bushes down flat, Hannah and Jack stared down at the hole.

"What do you think this is?" he asked.

"Get your knife out of that bag of yours."

Taking the knife from Jack, Hannah started scraping away some of the grass and moss surrounding the hole. "Can you find me a nice thick branch that we can use as a shovel?"

Within seconds, a real collapsible shovel was shoved into Hannah's hand. When Hannah looked up at Jack, he just shrugged his shoulders and pointed to his pink backpack.

After a few minutes of scraping and shoveling, Hannah and Jack managed to uncover a good portion of the hole.

"It looks like the remains of a campfire—an old one. Maybe this area was also occupied by the same aboriginal group we're excavating," Hannah suggested.

"Probably." Jack looked up towards the smaller cliff face. "If someone camped out here, I wonder about this second cliff face. It kinda looks out of place somehow."

Jack wandered down through the high grass, slowly making his way towards the unusual rock. "I'm surprised no one ever noticed this place."

"I think it's hard to see it when you're down on the beach. The trees are in the way. It's only once you're up here and got past those bent trees that you get a really good look at this cliff."

"Come look at this Hannah," Jack yelled excitedly, beckoning Hannah over to where he was standing. As Hannah reached her friend, she cried out. He was gone. One minute he was standing there, partially hidden by overgrown chokecherry bushes. The next minute he was gone.

"Jack! Jack! Where'd you go? Stop fooling around!"

"I'm right here!" Sure enough, Jack was once again standing right in front of Hannah, seeming to grow out of the bushes. His eyes were bulging, and he had a huge grin on his face.

"Hannah, from what I can see, we've just found ourselves a fantastic cave! Get me my bag. We're going spelunking!"

Chapter 13

Miraculous Recovery

Spelunking! Super...wonderful...and can you believe it's all done in the dark, with great big walls slowly closing in on you. Hannah was muttering to herself. She was not exactly enthusiastic about a journey down into the depths of the earth. Better yet, she was not going.

"I'll stand guard outside here while you go exploring," Hannah suggested, glancing inside the cave. The cliff face had turned out to have a very well-hidden entrance. It was covered with yards of hanging bushes and a gold mine of cobwebs, and Jack had to use a stick to get rid of as much of the fine silk threads as he could.

"Nah, I think you'd be better off sticking close to me," Jack replied. "You never know who might just drop in and kidnap you."

"Get real! This is PEI," Hannah scoffed at

the idea of anything dangerous happening on her island.

"So it's just our imagination that we have police breathing down our necks, and bad guys stealing golden armbands, right?"

No comment.

"How many flashlights did you bring in that pink bag of yours?"

"One."

"One?"

"One."

"Oh."

"We'll share it. I'm good with sharing."

With a heavy sigh, Hannah followed Jack inside the cave. The entrance was a very narrow opening that looked like a natural crack in the cliff. Much of it had been hidden by the bushes, but Jack's sharp eyes had spotted an unnaturally dark line among all the green plants. When he got up close to it, he noticed a slight breeze on his face. Following the cool current of air, Jack discovered the crack and squeezed through it to explore.

"Are the batteries good?"

"Fresh from the package."

"Do you have extras?"

"Of course. Who do you think I am?"

"Where are they?"

"Can you stop harping on the stupid flashlight? Enjoy the show! It's not everyday you get to explore a secret cave."

"Must be my lucky day," Hannah sighed, following Jack through the cave's opening.

Once inside, Hannah felt fresh air blowing on her sweaty skin. She had the impression of being in a larger space than expected. Jack turned on his flashlight and directed the strong beam around the rough walls. Hannah noticed small trickles of water glinting off the beam of light, probably the same streams that flowed down the outside of the rocky outcropping they were on. The floor was actually rather smooth, and covered with fine red sand.

Hannah spied something interesting in the flashlight's beam. Symmetrical lines were carved into some of the cave walls. Hannah ran her hand over these lines but could not make out whether they were natural or deliberate. At a glance they looked like drawings of some kind, but time and erosion had taken their toll on whatever was here.

"Look Hannah, the cave opens up into a passageway."

"Yippee! Now let's go. I've seen enough."

"Come on. I'll lead the way."

Another sigh. Hannah grabbed the back of Jack's shirt, stepping on his heels a couple of times as she followed him down the tunnel. The walls were narrow but not too bad. Hannah was able to extend her arms straight out her sides and just barely brushed her fingertips against the sandy rock. Another bonus was that they didn't have to stoop through the tunnels. Hannah hated low ceilings even more than caves.

"How long is this tunnel?" Hannah felt like she had been walking for hours.

"Don't know, but we seem to be going down. Do you feel it?"

"Yeah. We've been walking for at least five minutes. We might actually be below sea level. I'm not sure I like the thought of all that water being on top of us—and these walls around us—and this floor under us. I feel kinda closed in."

"Whoa! Why'd ya stop so suddenly? You ripped my shirt!"

"Sorry, but did you hear that?"

"Hear what?"

"It sounded like small rocks falling behind us."

"That probably happens all the time," Jack explained. "Rocks crumble, especially this soft sandstone."

"That's comforting, considering we're surrounded by the stuff," Hannah wheezed.

"Don't worry about it." Jack turned to face Hannah. "From the looks of this place, it's been around for a very long time. I'm sure it'll last a bit longer while we explore. Come on. I can't wait to see what's at the end of this place."

They continued to meander down the tunnel, turning right and left several times as they snaked their way further down. Every once in a while Hannah heard falling pebbles slithering down somewhere farther back up the tunnel. She forced herself to ignore it.

Suddenly, Jack's flashlight dimmed.

"What's happening, Jack?"

"We're out of the tunnel. Don't you feel it?"

"Now that you mention it, yeah, I do."

Jack's flashlight beam was definitely not as bright as it was in the smaller space of the tunnel. Hannah saw that they were now in a cavern, and boy, was it big. Jack's light simply disappeared when he pointed it straight ahead; only illuminating what was immediately close by.

"Jack? By any chance, do you have any candles in your bag?"

"Of course! Who do you think I am?"

Hannah had a good look around after Jack lit one of his white utility candles.

They were standing in the bottom of a giant cavern. Around and above them rose wide ledges that disappeared into the darkness. Hannah walked over to the ledge on her left. Many rocks had tumbled down over time, but she scrambled over them to reach the top of the ledge nearest her.

Hannah observed that these ledges were quite deep. With the weak light coming from the candle, she could not see all that far. Walking a bit away from the ledge, she came upon a set of shallow steps. When she reached the top, she raised the candle above her head for better light. A series of six natural stone columns formed some kind of rectangular structure. Unlike the red stone that made up the cave, these columns were white and had four very smooth square sides. As Hannah brought her candle closer, she noticed that there were pictures carved onto their sides. As she neared the closest of the six columns, she saw images of snakes twisting around and up the column. Jack saw them, too, and whistled!

"Wow!"

"They're not snakes, but sea creatures," Hannah whispered. "And all sorts. They're beautiful. Jack, don't these sea serpents look similar to the one on the armband? It looks like the same style to me. And what do you think the rock is made of? It's really smooth. I bet its marble! Just like the artifact Mr. Mac found."

A huge rock stood in the centre of the columns. Hannah walked up to it and ran her fingers across the flat top. The candle's flickering flames illuminated more of these sea creatures. Maybe the rock was an altar of some sort. Looking up, Hannah lost sight of the columns after about twenty feet up. She had no idea how high they rose but the cavern's ceiling stretched away into darkness.

"Holy moley, will you look at this!" Jack shouted, pointing off to the right. Quickly, he scrambled back down the ledge and onto the cavern's floor. Following Jack's flashlight beam, Hannah ran up to her friend and stared, speechless.

"Jack? What is this?"

"What do you think?"

"It looks like a boat."

"A big one!"

"Look at the prow..."

"I'm looking."

"It's the same creature that's on the armband, only 3-D."

"Yup!"

"Do you think we found Atlantis?"

"Yup!"

"Oh my!"

"Yup! Yup!"

The boat was at least thirty feet long. Made of rough hewn wooden planks, it looked sleek and fast. It reminded Hannah of the Viking boat she once saw in Ottawa's Museum of Civilization. However, unlike those Viking boats, this one had some sort of structure built into it, towards the stern of the boat. Although most of this structure was long gone, what was left looked like a shelter, perhaps used during rainy weather. Its roof, probably made from animal skins or cloth, had long since rotted away, but some of the posts that had held up the covering were still in place.

"Careful there," Jack warned Hannah as she climbed some of the surrounding rocks to get a better look inside.

"The boat looks like it was deliberately docked here." Jack looked up at Hannah. Pointing to the group of rocks surrounding the ridged bottom of the boat, he continued. "Those rocks were put down there to keep the boat from tilting off to the side. Quite smart actually, since wood rots away over time, but stone lasts forever. Do you think it was a ceremonial vessel or something?"

"No, I don't." Hannah shook her head. "Look at the sides of the boat. You can see a faint line going all the way around the boat. That's a waterline. This boat was definitely used in water. The boards are much paler above that line."

"How'd it get in here, I wonder?" Jack continued circling the boat.

"Remember what Izzy said." Hannah ran her fingers along the boat's waterline. "About 9000 years ago, this was still above water. The cave must've opened out to the sea. It looks like it was a natural protected harbour. I bet the opening that led out to the sea was sealed up somehow, either by accident or on purpose. And even though all this is now underwater, the seal made it watertight! Do you feel how dry it is in here?"

Jack nodded. "I get you, Hannah. Now that the opening is underwater, people eventually forgot this place ever existed. Izzy mentioned groups of people living here a long time ago, but they disappeared without a trace. Probably the rising sea level just buried their homes. "

Looking around, it suddenly hit her. The ledge, the cavern bottom. It all made sense. "Jack, I think I know how they got the boat in here. The bottom of the cavern was actually like a canal, filled with water. The water must have come right up close to the top of the ledges that go all around the cavern. People stepped off the boats right on to the ledges. Like we said before, a natural harbour."

While Hannah was talking, Jack made his way up the other side of the boat, using some of the rocks strewn around as stepping stones. He shone his flashlight inside the prow of the boat. Suddenly he called out to Hannah, who was still looking around the stern.

"There's something in here! I'm going in!"

"Be careful Jack," Hannah warned. "This boat is not as strong as it looks. Some of the boards look like they'll turn to dust! Don't fall through the wood. I don't want this artifact damaged."

"What about damaging me?"

"Not important!"

"Thanks."

"No problem. What do you see?"

"It's some sort of bundle," he cried excitedly.

"Something's wrapped up in some deerskin."

"Open it!"

"The deerskin is in really bad shape," Jack explained. "I'm afraid it's going to fall apart when I open it up."

"Do your best."

"Okay. Here I go..."

Hannah heard a sudden intake of breath.

"Whoohoo! Hannah! You gotta see this!"

Scrambling across the boat, Hannah carefully slipped in beside Jack and stared down at the bundle.

"It's the other armband we've been looking for," she whispered. "And these other things beside it, they look like they're also made of gold. What are they?"

"Statues." Jack gingerly reached out and picked up one of the heavy figures, turning it around and studying the intricate spirals carved into the deep yellow gold. The statues measured about ten inches and seemed to weigh a ton.

"This one looks like it's a mix of human and sea animal. Look, it's got the face of a bearded man, but the body of a fish. He's holding a pitchfork. He looks an awful lot like one of the Greek gods I read about this year in English class."

"Poseidon." Hannah reached out to touch the gold. "And that's a trident in his hand."

"And this other one is a woman with long hair, some sort of headband around her head. She's human until we get to her legs, which look like the tentacles of a squid."

"That thing around her head might be a crown," Hannah pointed out. "This guy is also wearing one."

"The detailed carvings on these statues are amazing. I can't wait to show Izzy and get her ideas on this!"

"No need to wait! I'm here!"

"IZZY! WHAT'RE YOU DOING HERE?"

"Claiming what's mine," the old woman cackled. "Thanks for the prize. Now hand it over. And I ain't saying please, neither!"

Chapter 14

Hero Worship

"Izzy, what're you talking about?" Hannah was still dealing with the shock of the old woman's sudden appearance. Izzy almost scared her to death!

"Both of you heard me the first time! Don't act dumb, although in Jack's case, it's not a big leap."

"Huh?"

"Point made. Now hand over that there little bundle. That precious little armband will go quite nicely with the one I have right here."

Hannah looked up and saw Izzy patting her raincoat's pocket. She was standing on the same rock where Hannah first stood.

"You stole the armband?"

"Not physically, no," Izzy snorted. "I had some help. Now, for the last time, give me the damned gold!"

"I'd hold off on that for a bit," boomed another voice, coming from somewhere within the cavern.

"Now what?!" Jack cried.

"What the he—"

Turning suddenly, Izzy was caught off balance and tumbled down the rock she had been standing on seconds before. Luckily, she didn't have far to go. She managed to grab hold of one of the rocks and pulled herself up to a sitting position. "Who in tarnations is—oh, it's you! I told you to wait for me outside the cave."

"Why? So that I'd miss all the fun? I want my share of the treasure. In fact, I decided that I want it all. Forget the deal we had. It's now history."

From out of the dark a tall figure leaped up on the rock that Izzy was on just moments before. Hannah and Jack gasped in shock. It was Marcie's boyfriend! But even more shocking was what Hannah discovered in the glow of Jack's flashlight.

"ANDREW?"

"In person!" he sang. "Surprised to see me?"

"What're you doing here?" Hannah stammered. "You're supposed to be busy with your landscaping business and enjoying the Blue Lobster."

"Do you actually think I'd let you guys get away with leaving me with that crap of a house you called the Blue Lobster?" he shook his head. "I think I got a bum deal on that one, and I needed more compensation than what you Morgan jerks gave me. All that talk about treasure and gold— now that was more up my alley. And I had a very willing partner, right Izzy?"

The old woman glared at him from the bottom of the rock pile.

"But—"

"I wouldn't interrupt him," Hannah advised Jack. "He's got a weapon."

"You bet I do," Andrew snorted, patting his jacket's bulging side pocket. Hannah got a glimpse of a really big gun!

"But you're Marcie's boyfriend."

"Yeah, that was great cover. I knew you were in on this dig, so I decided to tag along. I found your pal Lucy's letter at the house."

"You broke into the Blue Lobster?" Hannah yelled. "That letter was left on the kitchen table. When did you do this?"

"Hannah, I wouldn't interrupt. Remember, he's got a gun," Jack whispered, yanking Hannah back down.

"Hmmm. Let's see. I think I paid a little visit

to *my* house the day after you got to the island. Remember, I've been here awhile now, scoping out some business possibilities. And that letter gave me some brilliant ideas. I started working on a plan right then and there! So, I've been keeping a close eye on you kids."

"Are you kidding me? You've been following us this whole time!" Hannah cried.

"I had to stick to you like glue, but I couldn't exactly join the dig team—couldn't afford to have you recognize me after all. So pretended I was dating Marcie. That was the hard part. She's way too nice. Yuck! Then Izzy came to me and offered me a deal to get in on this treasure hunt. That was more like it."

"Izzy was in on this all along?" Hannah gasped.

"You bet I was," snapped Izzy, still struggling to sit up on one of the lower rocks. She kept rubbing her left ankle. "Does it look like this idiot's got much brain power behind all that dark hair? I suspected right from the start that he wasn't tagging along with Marcie for the sake of romance. Scumbags like him never do. He's an opportunist. So I sweetened the pot with promises of shared treasure. In exchange, I let him know what I wanted. It's amazing the response you get when you talk about gold. He jumped just like I thought he would. What a jerk! I gave him the combination to the safe. He's the one who stole the armband out of the truck when he was down there visiting Marcie."

"But the box was sealed with special tape," Jack interrupted.

"Boy, who do you think you're dealing with?" Izzy shrieked. "I gave Andrew the tape I used to seal the box, since he had to cut the first seal to get the armband out. He resealed it with new tape. That's why Charlie told the police that the seal wasn't cut when he took the box out at the university. The only glitch in this brilliant plan was you kids. You took your fluffin' time leaving the Cavendish dig, and Andrew got antsy and made an early appearance. Lucky he was far enough away that you didn't see his mug."

"Was Charlie in on this too?" Jack asked.

"Charlie Bones was just a poor schmuck who fell for a free Timmy's coffee." Izzy shook her head as she resumed. "I told the big oaf over here to treat him to some coffee when he came to pick Marcie up in Cavendish that fateful day. Charlie's coffee was spiked with some laxatives."

"Poop medicine?!"

"You're too crude, Jackie dear," Izzy frowned. "Mind your manners, hon. Anyway, Andrew told Marcie he had seen some trespassers walking around the dig site and told her to do a final walk-through. You know, make sure everything's okey dokey. Charlie was supposed to be waiting for her in the truck, guarding the armband. However, the call of nature hit him like a four ton truck, and he had to find a bathroom real fast. A lot of laxatives in that coffee! Of course, with both Charlie and Marcie gone, the truck was there for the taking. That's when Andrew got the armband out of the safe."

"Why didn't Charlie tell the police that he was gone for a bit?"

"Don't know. Probably embarrassed about the bathroom issue. And he still wouldn't be able to prove that he wasn't the one who took the armband. After all, he was alone while Marcie was off checking on the dig site. No one knew about Andrew being around."

"Emily did!" cried Hannah.

"And no one believed her! No one ever believes kids. Good thing for me, or else this whole fiasco could have fallen apart. Now, Andrew, help me up and let's get out of here. I think I twisted my ankle when I fell. We'll discuss our *deal* as we're heading out."

Another booming laugh, "You're staying here with the kids, you old bat. I need time to make my getaway, and you'll just crimp my style. Besides, I ain't the type to share. I told you before, the treasure's all mine now."

Izzy was furious. She was shaking with anger, and her face turned a frightening brick red. Hannah watched wide-eyed as the old woman pulled herself up to a standing position.

"I ain't going to let a piece of dirt like you take what took me an entire lifetime to find!" she spat.

Andrew shrugged his shoulders and pulled out his gun, pointing it at the threesome. "Don't do anything stupid, although I wouldn't put it past anyone of you!" He quickly reached behind him and picked up a bright pink backpack.

"Hey, that's mine," Jack yelled.

"Really? I thought it was Hannah's. Okay, let's see what's in here that I could use to tie you three up."

A few seconds later Andrew pulled out some yellow nylon rope.

"How perfect can you get?!?!"

"You *had* to be prepared, didn't you?" Hannah glared at Jack.

"What if we fell in a hole and had to be hauled up?"

"Who would do the hauling if we're both in the same hole?"

Minutes later, Jack, Hannah, and Izzy had their hands and feet tied up. The offending pink backpack was left leaning against the ancient boat. Jack's flashlight, now lying beside the backpack, was still on and pointed at the trio.

"Have a great evening, folks. Sorry I can't stay longer, but I got places to see, things to do. You understand?"

"This is not the end," Jack yelled at Andrew's retreating back. "We know where to find you!"

No response.

"I can't believe he left us." Jack looked back at his female companions.

"I can't believe he took the armband out of my pocket and left me here with you two idiots." Izzy shifted, trying to get more comfortable.

"And *I* can't believe you're a thief and a liar," Hannah spat at the old woman. "You betrayed us. How could you do that? We looked up to you...

and here we were, so worried about you having your heart attack."

"It wasn't really a heart attack. Just a bit of a spell, is all," Izzy said. "Nothing serious, my lovies. And those sweet young doctors fixed me up all nice and fancy-like with their procedures and medicines."

"How'd you get away from the hospital?" Jack asked, always curious.

"Oh, that was a piece of cake. I finally managed to light my cigar and waved it under one of them smoke detectors they have all over the place. It was a riot, what with all them patients running around in their nighties, their butts hanging out in plain sight. Don't think that place ever had a fire drill before, so it was pure chaos. I managed to slip away without anyone knowing or seeing. They were all too busy trying to get the patients on life support out of the building in one piece. Hilarious."

"But Izzy, why'd you do all this? I don't get it? It's pure evil." Hannah looked over at Izzy, who was still smiling.

"Why? Why? I'll tell you why! I've worked hard all my life, looking for the tiniest bit of recognition. Do you know how many *other* people have taken credit for my discoveries? It's always the people who pay for the damned digs that come out being famous...*and* rich! Yeah, I wrote some great papers, and my reputation as a teacher is second to none. But I wanted the gold! I wanted that major discovery that would put me on the map. Can you imagine what life would be like for the person who actually found Atlantis?"

"Is that all you can think about? Fame and fortune?" Jack shook his head in disgust.

"You bet your cute little bottom," Izzy snapped, wiggling around a bit trying to loosen the ropes. "What else is there to live for at my age, other than those handsome young doctors who waited on me hand and foot? I wanted to make sure I'd be remembered, and my name would be on everyone's lips!"

"Oh, for sure you'll be the talk of the island! But not in a good way." Hannah twisted around, looking at Jack's backpack.

"Do you think someone's looking for us?" Jack asked.

"They might start wondering where we are, and why we're not back yet," Hannah hoped. She was slowly scooting her way towards the backpack, dragging her feet through the pebbly earth as she went. She leaned against one of the rocks supporting the boat, and in a great act of precision balancing, managed to turn herself on her knees, bounced forward and back a couple of times, and then with a great big grunt, heaved herself up to a standing position...then fell back.

Jack laughed. "Smooth!"

"Shut up!"

"I'm hearing that a lot lately."

"And yet you're not getting the message!"

Hannah went through the whole dragging and grunting process again, but this time managed to remain standing. With her ankles and wrists still tied, she hopped towards the pink bag and turned to face Jack and Izzy. A couple of fancy moves later, she had Jack's bag gripped tightly in her hands.

"This would be so much easier if my hands were tied in front of me," she panted as she hopped back to Jack.

"This would be a piece of cake if our hands weren't tied at all," Jack gave Izzy a very dirty look.

Hannah glanced at Jack. "You know, you're flexible enough. I bet if you strained your little muscles a tad bit, you could pull your legs through your arms. That way, at least you'll have your hands in front of you."

"What do you want out of the bag?" Jack asked while he dragged his hands under his buttocks. With a sudden jerk he had his hands out in front of him. "Now what?"

"Now you can cut everyone's ropes with your handy dandy Swiss Army knife," said Hannah. She struggled to get Jack's knife from within the folds of his bag.

"I hate to admit it, but lucky you were prepared. Now cut!"

"What about her?" Jack asked, eyeing Izzy as he finished cutting through the last of Hannah's ropes.

"What about her?" Hannah returned the favour and sliced away the ropes tying Jack's hands and feet. Then she checked the flashlight, while Jack rummaged through his bag, looking for the extra batteries.

"Well, do we just leave her here or what?"

"Good question."

"I mean, she's evil, you know."

"Listen up, you twits! I might be old, but I certainly ain't deaf!" Izzy shouted.

Ignoring the old woman, Jack continued to think. "Yeah, but we need to turn her over to the authorities—hey, what's that?"

Suddenly, a great big boom crashed through

the cavern and shook the earth. Jack fell heavily against Hannah and both kids went tumbling to the ground beside Izzy. A series of smaller booms followed the first one, and then silence. Seconds later a billowy cloud of red dust and pebbles poured down from the tunnel entrance.

"Are you okay?" Jack coughed.

"Yeah. Ouch! I think I'm good," Hannah wheezed. "But I'll be even better when you get off me."

"Oops, sorry."

"What do you think that was?" Hannah brushed off some of the dirt from her face.

"It sounded like explosions," Izzy spoke up. "And I'm just great, too, by the way."

"We didn't ask," Jack said.

"My point exactly," Izzy snapped.

"Do you think Andrew set off that explosion to block us in?" Hannah got up and headed toward the tunnel entrance, carrying the flashlight in front of her.

"I'd say that was one of your more intelligent guesses," said Izzy. "Question is: where'd he get the explosives? I seriously doubt he came prepared with a bomb. But it didn't sound like a natural cave-in. So what else could he have used?"

"Ahem..."

Hannah and Izzy turned towards Jack, who had his hand up high.

"Well...I had...or...he must have found...boy oh boy!"

"Spit it out Jack!" Hannah stormed back to where Jack was standing, hands on her hips, waiting for an answer.

"Okay, okay. I had some fireworks in my bag. He must have taken them out after he tied us up. We had our backs to him, remember? I heard the rummaging, but I never thought—"

"Fireworks? Fireworks? Whatever for?"

"Well, if we decided to stay out late while looking for Emily, we could have had a romantic evening on the beach, capped off by a wonderful display of fireworks. I got them from my uncle and was saving them for a special occasion. Guess this was it."

"Oh."

"Okay, enough of this lovey dovey crap, dumb-dumbs. How many sticks did you have?" Izzy's glare pinned Jack to the spot.

"Ummm, I guess, well, let's see...one...three, oh yeah, forgot that one...huh...seven, eight...Oh! I think I had ten sticks...or a bit more. And maybe some extra fuses so that I could hook them up and light them from a distance. I didn't want to be blown to bits, you know. Better safe than sorry, I say!"

"Ten? Ten?? TEN?????" Hannah cried. "We're trapped! Oh my god! My worst nightmare come true."

"Get a hold of yourself, you big old nincompoop," snapped Izzy. "In a tunnel this size, the explosion from ten sticks of fireworks would be big enough to bring down some rocks but not the whole tunnel. They're not sticks of dynamite! One of you will have to go down the tunnel and check it out...see if it's blocked completely or only a bit."

"*Your* fireworks, so *you* do the honours." Hannah shoved the flashlight into Jack's dirty hands. She turned abruptly away from him, stomped off and sat down heavily next to the boat, as far from Izzy as she could get.

With a sigh, Jack limped off down the tunnel. To Hannah it seemed like he was gone for several years. However, after twenty minutes or so, Jack was back.

"What did you find, Jack? Is it blocked? Can we get out?"

"Yes and no, or at least not yet," he sighed again, sinking to the ground next to Hannah. "Part of the tunnel did cave in, but from what I could tell, we might be able to dig our way through by morning."

"You mean work all night?" Hannah groaned. Suddenly, she sat up straight. "Hey, maybe they'll send a rescue team. They must've heard the explosion. We're not that far from camp."

"True, but they won't be able to pinpoint the exact spot where the explosion came from, or where we went into the cave. Remember how well it was hidden, even from us? We had to get up close to it. And we found it in bright sunshine. It's gonna be kinda hard to find in the dark."

Hannah turned to Izzy. "How did you find us?"

"We followed you. Saw your every move. Lucky thing we did, otherwise I never would've found that crack in the cliff."

Hannah slumped back on the rock. "Party-pooper."

After debating the issue, Hannah and Jack decided to leave Izzy in the cavern. They didn't feel up to the challenge of dragging a complaining and mean old woman through the tunnels, and Hannah thought Izzy was better off resting where she was. She was looking a bit ragged again, despite her protests.

Before they left, Jack and Hannah set about building a small fire for Izzy. There was a nice supply of driftwood lying around throughout the cavern, probably gathered by the ancient people who had once stayed there. Lucky for Izzy that Jack had packed more than enough matches to light his fireworks and candles.

"Did you check her ropes?" Jack looked back at Hannah as they slowly made their way back up the tunnel, trying to avoid the larger rocks that had rolled down after the explosion.

"Yup. Tight as can be."

"I'm beginning to think that all that money your parents spent on sending you to Boy Scouts is really paying off big time."

"Thanks...a compliment. Wow. We're finally bonding. Anyway, those knots needed to be tight, because I don't trust Izzy. She double crossed us the whole time we were on these digs. In my books, she's a traitor. And I don't want her sneaking down the tunnel after us and whacking me on the head as she makes her great escape."

"Well have no fear," Hannah laughed. "She's not going anywhere fast."

Finally they reached the blockage. Jack pointed his flashlight at the mountain of rocks that blocked the tunnel.

"How many extra batteries do you have?" Hannah gulped.

"Not enough."

"Great. What now?"

"We work fast."

"Okay. Technically, we only need to dig a hole wide enough for one of us to fit through, right? And there's already a small opening right there at the top of the pile."

"Actually, it's quite tiny."

"My point is we already have a head start with that hole up there."

"Extremely unrealistic optimism. I like that in a girl."

"I need a lot of it being around you! Okay! Let's start digging."

The going was disappointingly slow. After they scraped off the first layer of dirt, they found that the piled up rocks were actually quite large and very heavy to move. The cave-in was also deeper than what they had first thought. Despite pulling away hundreds of pounds of rocks, it didn't look like they had made much progress.

"Jack, the flashlight's beginning to get dim."

"Yeah, I know. But I'll squeeze every last juice of power out of it before I put the other batteries in there."

"What time is it?"

"Don't know. I cracked my watch during the explosion. Just keep digging. Time flies when you're having fun, right?"

Ten minutes later the flashlight went dead and Jack replaced the old batteries with the last of the new ones.

"It must be late," Hannah panted, pushing down a particularly large rock away from the slowly growing hole. "I think we should rest a bit."

"If we take a break, we'll have to turn off the flashlight. No use leaving it on if we're not doing anything."

Hannah took a deep breath. "Alright. But wait till I get down from here. I want to get comfortable before you turn it off."

Sitting down next to Jack, Hannah leaned her head back against the rough tunnel wall, took another deep breath, and closed her eyes. "Ready when you are."

Click.

The darkness was intense. When Hannah worked up enough courage to open her eyes, she couldn't see the hand she held an inch from her nose. With little else to do, Hannah decided to rest her eyes a bit. Within minutes she was asleep, her head rolling slowly towards Jack's shoulder. A few minutes after that, Jack's flashlight dropped into his lap, and he, too, was fast asleep.

Chapter 15

Scout's Honour

Hannah had a funny dream. She was in her new house, Just Peachy. She was painting her bedroom walls (lime green, of course!) when suddenly a pirate looking an awfully lot like Jack Sparrow, popped up outside her window. Hannah screamed. Jack Sparrow screamed. Hannah stuck her tongue out at him. Jack Sparrow stuck his finger up his nose. Then she heard pounding on her door. Oh no! Who could it be? Should she open the door?

"Wakey wakey, eggs and bakey," cried a voice beyond the door. The pounding continued, but now her whole room was moving!

"Hannah, Hannah, wake up," Jack cried.

"Jack Sparrow, leave me alone, you pirate, you!" Hannah mumbled, batting away Jack's hands.

"Hannah, you're being rescued! You gotta wake up for that!"

"Wha—? What's going on? What're you talking about? Is it time to dig again?"

"Nope! No more digging for the two of you." Lucy turned and shook Jack awake too.

"Go 'way," he moaned. "Pookie bear! Where's my Pookie pie?"

"Jacko! Wake up. It's morning! Wayne Simpson and Dr. Williams are here. They're on the other side of the cave-in. Can't you hear the pounding?"

With bleary eyes, Hannah and Jack tried to focus on Lucy. Suddenly, Hannah realized where she was.

"Lucy! It was Andrew!' she shrieked. "He trapped us in here. You have to call the police. We can't let him get away!"

"It's horrible! He was behind the theft of the armband, along with Izzy," Jack added. He patted down his cowlick, but no matter how much spit he put on the annoying clump of hair, it bounced right back up on the top of his head.

"Hannah! Hannah! Guess what? I'm here, too!" Suddenly, Emily's face poked through the hole that Hannah and Jack had been working on the night before. "We were so worried about you and Jack! Mr. Wayne and Lucy found me in the woods. I think they were worried that I was lost, which I was a bit, but that's beside the point. Anyways...after we all got together and had a group hug, we decided to go look for you guys on the beach. Just as we were coming out of the woods, guess who we saw? Marcie's boyfriend. But up close he was really Andrew! I recognized him. I shouted, *Andrew,* but he ran. What a klutz. He ran right smack dab into the middle of our dig site. Fell in a pit and broke his ankle right then and there. When we found him, he had all this gold on him, including the armbands that looked a lot like what we found in Cavendish."

Hannah groaned. It was way too early to listen to Emily.

"Did you call the police?" Jack asked.

"Course we did. Who do you think we are?" By now the Emzo had pushed herself through the quickly widening hole and jumped down to where Jack and Hannah were standing. They were soon joined by Wayne Simpson and Dr. Williams.

"How'd you know where to find us?" Jack asked, still working on his cowlick.

"Picked up your garbage!"

Jack and Hannah shot puzzled looks at Mr. Wayne.

"You left your sleeping bag at the bottom of

some rocks," Emily interrupted. "We also found your suntan lotion, pillow, and wind-up radio."

"I sure could've used them last night," he murmured.

"We're going to need to go back and get Izzy." Hannah quickly explained what had happened last night.

"Yeah, we got some of that crappy story from that idiot Andrew," Wayne snorted. "He spilled his guts to the police, blaming it all on the old bat. What a gentleman! We knew she was gone from the hospital, but we all thought she was kidnapped or something. I still can't believe she was in on this!"

"In on it? *In on it*! She was the mastermind of the whole thing! She used poor Marcie and Charlie to get what she wanted. Greedy old bat!"

The rescue team had brought enough flash-lights for everyone, and they carefully made their way back down the tunnel. When they entered the cavern, everyone came to a sudden stop and stared. More flashlights meant more light, and Hannah could make out more detail she had missed the night before. An incredible sight! The walls closest to her had intricate images etched into them: Ships sailing on rough waters, men fishing from their prows; Poseidon surrounded by sea creatures. And then there was the gold! Small niches, or holes in the walls above the ledges, contained more golden statues just like the ones in the boat."

"We missed all this!" Jack whispered in awe.

"Good thing we did, or else Andrew would've taken them, too!" Hannah reluctantly turned away from the gold and looked towards the boat where they had left Izzy. The fire from last night had died down, and only a few embers glowed among the ashes. Jack's bag was lying not far from the boat, but Hannah saw no signs of Izzy. Where was she? She couldn't have gone far tied up the way she was.

As Hannah approached the fire, she noticed bunches of yellow rope scattered around the ashes. Bending down, she picked up some of the ropes and examined the ends. They looked like they had been melted! Oh no!!!

"IZZY'S ESCAPED!!!!" Hannah was quickly joined by the others. "Look at the ropes. She must have used the fire to burn through them. OH MY GOD! SHE COULD BE HIDING ANYWHERE IN THE CAVERN!!!"

"But how could she see in the dark?" Jack asked. "We had the only flashlight."

"We never searched her, did we? Neither did Andrew. We know she had a flashlight when she first found us, but it must have rolled away when she fell off the rocks. It probably got knocked out when it hit the floor, but she most likely got it going again."

Hannah was still agitated. "So she had light! Great! But she couldn't have gotten out. The only way out is through the tunnel, and we were in that tunnel. Even if she snuck by us when we were sleeping, she still would've been stuck. The hole wasn't big enough for her to crawl through yet."

"Hannah, calm down. We'll find her." Dr. Williams placed his hand on Hannah's shoulder.

Jack got the fire going again, hoping that the flames would give them extra light. Dr. Williams quickly discussed plans to search the cavern. Wayne took Hannah and Jack and searched the left side of the cavern, while Dr. Williams went with Emily and Lucy and scoured the right side. After a quick look, everyone gathered back round the fire.

"There's no sign of her," Lucy said, gently rubbing her forehead. She had bumped it against a rock when she had bent to examine some footprints. Unfortunately, the footprints disappeared when they reached a pile of tumbled boulders. "She must've made her way up that ledge. I looked for signs of her, but found nothing. She's got to be there though because that's where her prints disappear."

"Where could she have gone? There're no other exits!" Jack smacked his hand against his thigh.

"Maybe there is one but we just haven't found it yet," Dr. Williams suggested.

"Even if there was an exit, wouldn't it just lead to the sea? I mean, this cave must be underwater," Hannah pointed out.

"Not necessarily," Dr. Williams said, rubbing his chin in thought. "I think perhaps the main entrance to this place must now be under water, but that doesn't mean this entire place is. Who's to say that there aren't any other tunnels that double back and lead to an exit? There must be more than one way in and out of here."

"I've got an idea!" Jack jumped up and ran to his bag. Seconds later he was holding a bottle of baby oil.

"What on earth is that for?" Lucy asked.

"I use this in case the suntan lotion doesn't work too well. It soothes my baby smooth skin after a burn," Jack explained.

"Oh brother," Lucy rolled her eyes. "Thanks for the info, but what I meant is why do you need it now?"

"My beautiful doubting Lucy, I will demonstrate to you how smart I am—and then for sure you'll fall madly in love with the hero that saved the day."

Smack!

"D'ya ever learn, laddie?" Wayne chuckled.

Ignoring the dull throbbing on the back of his head, Jack fetched a piece of driftwood, tore up his pillowcase into long strips, and squirted loads of baby oil on each piece of cotton, soaking the material. Then he wrapped the pieces around the driftwood and lit it.

"Voila! A torch. Nice and smoky. We'll go back to the last place Lucy saw Izzy's footprints and pass this torch over the area. Technically, if we find an opening, there'll be fresh air coming out of it, blowing the smoke away from the torch."

"I get it! Your torch will 'see' the opening where Izzy disappeared through before our eyes do!" Emily clapped her hands. "Let's go."

"Ya know, candles would've worked just as well," Wayne pointed out.

"Yeah, I know," laughed Jack, "But then the

girls wouldn't have been awed by my sheer talent for invention under pressure."

Everyone watched as Jack walked back and forth, waving his torch near where Lucy had first seen the footprints. Tense minutes ticked away. Finally, Jack stopped in front of a small cave-in.

"Look at the smoke," Emily whispered. "It's blowing back towards us.

"I see a small opening," Hannah peered in a small, dark hole. It was almost covered by fallen rocks, probably from a cave-in. "But the hole's way too small for Izzy to escape through."

"But look at the ground," Dr. Williams pointed down. "There's long gouge marks from that end of the cave to here. I bet Izzy found this opening and then dragged these rocks over here, trying to hide the hole. It was an Izzy-made cave in. Not natural at all."

"That mustn't have been easy," Lucy mused.

"No, but Izzy is an archaeologist—if nothing else, she knows her rocks!" Dr. Williams said. "Sadly, she's a sneaky one."

They all took turns bending down and shining their flashlights through the hole. After removing most of the rocks, the team discovered another tunnel similar in size and shape to the one first discovered by Jack and Hannah.

"We need to get down there and follow her," Jack shouldered his way in. Suddenly he was grabbed from behind by Dr. Williams.

"No one's going down there unarmed," he shook his head.

"Besides, Izzy's probably long gone. And we need back up. Preserving this site is more important right now than chasing some crazy old woman. We'll let the police do their job and get her. In the meantime, I'll head back up and get some help. Wayne, you stay here just in case the old coot decides to come back for another visit. We don't want her stealing all these priceless artifacts. We'll survey this site the professional way and record everything we see. We've just made history and damned if I'm going to screw this up!"

"Spoken like a true archaeologist!" Wayne nodded. Rubbing his hands together, he spoke again. "Let's put this plan into action. Now who's staying with me?"

The four friends looked at each other. In silent agreement, they all decided to stay. Jack spoke up for his friends.

"Damned if we're going to miss a minute of this! Just make sure you bring back some breakfast, sir. I'm starving!"

Chapter 16

All this Hullabaloo

Hours later the dig crew had brought in powerful halogen lights and the entire cave was lit up. The archaeologists were documenting the site, and RCMP police officers snapped photographs of the crime scene. A team of officers, escorted by Dr. Williams, made their way through the tunnel where Izzy was thought to have disappeared. The tunnel meandered around the inside of the cliff until it finally opened up to the outside world. Sure enough, no Izzy was anywhere to be found.

Once Dr. Williams got back to the cavern he explained, "We came out about fifty yards farther down the beach, through an opening like what Jack and Hannah found yesterday. It wasn't easy for anyone as big as me, but Izzy wouldn't have had a problem scrambling through the exit. It's a pretty small hole, but she's a pretty small lady. I bet she's long gone now. The police have an APB—"

"APB?" asked Emily.

Flashes from multiple cameras were still going off throughout the cavern, and voices were raised in excitement. Word was quickly getting around about the amazing discovery.

"All Points Bulletin, Emily." Dr. Williams continued. "Everyone's looking for her. Her picture is being circulated to all stores, as well as the Confederation Bridge people, and ferry operators, just in case she decides to try and leave the island. Don't worry. They'll get her. After all, we're a tiny island. Where could she go?

"In the meantime, Andrew is safely locked up and is facing charges here on the island. You won't see him for a while."

"He's in big doo doo," Emily laughed. Looking around the cavern, Emily noticed Marcie directing workers here and there. One of those workers, Wayne Simpson of all people, gave her a squinty look, but nonetheless, still picked up the wheelbarrow and pushed it to the far end of the cavern. Dr. Williams had also been following this exchange and turned back to his little group.

"Marcie's in her element. She finally showed up this morning," Dr. Williams added. "She explained that she felt so bad about everything that was going on with this dig that she had to do something about it. She went looking for her boyfriend, Andrew, to ask for his help. Unfortunately she walked in on him cleaning his gun. Things didn't go well after that. He tied her up and dumped her in the trunk of her own car."

"Poor Marcie," Emily said. "Where'd she get to?"

"Andrew drove her car to a remote part of the Yankee Hill woods out in French River and left Marcie there. A couple of tourists luckily heard her shouts and managed to track her down."

"I think she's very relieved that the police no longer suspect her," Hannah said. "And I see Charlie is also back and helping out. Poor guy! At least he's recovered from that bout of laxatives. That was really cruel giving him that stuff just to get him away from the truck. And then setting Marcie up for the fall, using her like that by tricking her into thinking someone's in love with her."

Hannah struggled with Izzy's guilt, too. She had trusted the old woman, as did everyone else on the dig. She had looked up to Izzy, thinking her so smart and hip. How could Izzy get so swept up with all the greed of treasure hunting? She had let everyone down. And now she was gone who knows where. Hannah thought that the most fitting justice for Izzy was to be missing out on all the discoveries being made in the cavern. Izzy hadn't noticed all those golden statues nestled smugly in the wall niches. Lucky thing too! So far, the dig crew had found twelve niches, and ten of them held golden statues. Hannah guessed the other two niches were home to the golden figures they had found in the boat.

"Dr. Williams, why do you think those two figures, along with the armbands, were found in the boat, and not in the wall niches?" Hannah asked.

"I think that the boat served a ceremonial purpose. A long time ago it was a real seafaring vessel used by the people who first came to the island. We'll be able to do a radiocarbon test and find out a pretty accurate age of the boat. Did you notice the shelf tucked away in the sheltered corner of the boat?"

Jack shook his head. "We missed that! We were there, but Izzy happened on the scene so suddenly, we didn't have time to explore all of the boat. Hannah and I were also afraid of breaking it. The wood looked so dried out."

"Good thing you didn't walk around too much," Dr. Williams nodded. "The boat is fragile in places, but in other areas the wood is quite strong. Anyway, I was telling you about the shelf. Guess what was tucked away under it? Human remains."

"OH MY GOD! SOMEONE WAS MURDERED?!"

"No, Emily, nothing like that," Dr. Williams turned to Teeny One. "These bones look very old. They were laid out in a fetal position, a very ancient burial style. Tucked in between the bones were all sorts of artifacts made of gold. And the designs on these artifacts were the same as those found on the armbands. Coincidence? I don't think so. I think the armbands belonged to this ancient person, and someone simply returned them to its rightful owner."

Suddenly, Marcie and Wayne burst in on this little group by the fire. Marcie was carrying a tray. As she placed it down at their feet, Hannah noticed that both armbands were spread out on it. "Take a look at what we discovered! I was examining the armbands and saw that the sea serpent images on it were unusual."

"In what way?" Dr. Williams gently picked up one of the armbands while Marcie held the other.

"This one is the armband that Jack found. It

has the snake's head on one side and tail on the other. Both the head and tail come out from the main body of the armband. The piece that you're holding, Dr. Williams, looks like it has the body of the snake. We knew that the armband we found in Cavendish could actually come apart in two pieces. In fact, *both* armbands can be taken apart. Now, if we look at these four separate pieces, we can see a pattern."

"It looks like a puzzle of a snake," Emily exclaimed as she bent over the gold pieces.

"That's right Emily," Marcie nodded. "Look at this!" She picked up one of the armbands and one of the pieces held by Dr. Williams. With a small click, the two pieces snapped together. Then she did the same with the two other pieces. Finally, all four pieces were clicked together. Holding it up, Marcie asked, "What do you think this is?"

"A crown!"

Excited voices floated around the campfire.

"It was Wayne who figured it out! It seems he's good with puzzles."

Marcie put the crown on her head. "See, the sea serpent's head sticks up above the band of the crown, almost like the Egyptian head pieces we see on Pharaohs. The serpent's tail is at the back of the head. Since the second piece of the crown, the other armband, was found in the boat close to the skeletal remains, I think that we found the body of an ancient king or queen. The armbands, now a crown, belonged to it. The columns and altar that Hannah found could be a place of worship, and the statuettes in the wall niches, gods and goddesses. I think this entire cavern was once a place of worship for a very ancient culture. I know I'm jumping the gun with the dating of the cavern, and we'll know more after the carbon dating results come back, but I think we've finally discovered the first evidence of an ancient culture that lived on the island."

"The story that Izzy told us at the campfire," Hannah mused, "—she said that the legend of Yuma was passed on by the aboriginal people that lived here, and that it could be real. It could date back quite far."

"Yes, it could," Dr. Williams agreed. "Perhaps the various cultures that lived on the island took the armbands and used them for ceremonial purposes. Maybe the chief used the armbands as a symbol of power from the ancient spirits. These artifacts could also have been used as talisman, protecting the villages. That is why we found one of the armbands at the Cavendish dig site. That artifact was part of village life, with the spirits watching over the people."

"But the other armband, along with two of the golden statues, was here in the boat." Jack pointed out.

"I think that whatever village had the armbands last, returned the artifacts for a reason." Dr. Williams looked at Marcie. "Did you get a look at the wrappings that held those two statues in the boat?"

"Yes! The deer hide was in pretty bad shape, but some of the decorative beadwork was still in place. Some of the beads were made of glass. That means that whoever owned this wrapping had already met up with European explorers and traded for those beads. And the style of design dates back to the time of first contact between the native aboriginals and the Europeans. I bet carbon dating of the hide would confirm all this."

"First contact was not always peaceful," Dr. Williams mused. "Maybe something went wrong. The aboriginals could have come under attack, and the gold had to be hidden. Accidentally, one of the armbands stayed behind. The attack was sudden, and the young child wearing it never got a chance to give it back to whoever brought the rest of the pieces here."

"Who were these people who brought the golden pieces back?" Emily ran a small finger along the edge of the crown.

"Good question," Marcie said. "When the Europeans first landed on the island, they were greeted by the Mi'kmaq people. The ancestors of these people are still around today, mainly on reservations near Charlottetown and St. Peter's Bay. But there were other cultures here before the Mi'kmaqs, and as you know, they disappeared without a trace. But there is no reason to assume that these ancient groups died off completely. Perhaps some of those people joined up with the newer groups coming to the island. They married and were integrated within the new culture. But their older culture's stories, legends, and traditions, never died out completely. The stories were passed on, as were the artifacts."

"Wow, Hannah! You were right on track with your theories," Jack beamed at Hannah. "What a woman! Tough *and* smart."

Hannah blushed at the compliment.

Marcie smiled and continued. "We can even go as far as to say that the Vikings could have come to this island as well, and although they did not stay, perhaps one or two expedition members decided to live on here with the natives, mixing their blood with the aboriginals."

"Then we'd have blue-eyed native Americans!" Jack laughed.

"That's right," Marcie agreed. "They would be quite rare, but it is possible. And if we assume that this place dates back to the time of Atlantis, and that perhaps some of the survivors of that civilization made their way here from the Mediterranean, then we might have more fair haired and blue-eyed people who settled here. Eventually, after hundreds of years, they would have mixed in with darker individuals who had migrated from elsewhere. Cultures always mix.

"Too bad Izzy is missing all this," Emily sighed. "She was so into it all. I wonder where she went to. I hope they catch her because I don't trust her. I want to sleep at night without worrying about her sneaking up to my window and scratching at the screen, trying to get to me! "

"Emily, your window is on the second floor," Lucy laughed.

"I think she's a witch and could fly up and get me!"

There's always hope, Hannah said under her breath.

"She's an old lady. It's not like she has too much life left in her. How much damage can she do on the run anyway?"

"Hannah, that's so awful." Jack stared at Hannah, mouth hanging open. "I'm disappointed in you. I never thought you were so heartless. Kind of an exciting thought, though! What a woman you are, Hannah—totally unpredictable. I like that!"

Hannah and her friends worked on the dig with the archaeologists for another week. The media hung around the site, waiting for the next important discovery to be made. But Hannah knew that archaeology was a slow process. More time was spent photographing, recording, and surveying the site than in digging. It looked like this project would continue for years. And who knew what was still waiting to be discovered under the sands, or whether they'd ever see Izzy again.

Hannah turned to her friends and stared thoughtfully at her faithful followers. "You know, I have a feeling we're going to be seeing Izzy again. She's not the type to give up so easily. Something tells me we need to be careful."

"You mean watch our backs," Lucy said.

"Exactly," Hannah agreed. "We're not done with this one, folks. Not by a long shot."

Acknowledgements

No book would be complete without the help and kindness from a number of people. In my case, I am truly thankful for the continually rich source of material provided by my daughters, Kira and Emmalyn. Their unique take on everyday tragedies, such as bad hair days, no clothes to wear despite burgeoning closets, or the dreaded "vegetables for supper," inspire me in so many ways. On a more profound level, I owe a great deal to my husband, Daniel. You still make me laugh. BTW, your socks are alive and are attacking me! I'm afraid retaliation is now inevitable.

A huge thank-you goes out to my biggest fans, Mami and Dedi, otherwise known as my loving parents, Zoltan and Margit. Their endless support, through thick and thin, has helped make me into who I am today.

I am pleasantly surprised that after all the

things I have put Jenevra Wetmore through, she still speaks to me, so I thank her for that. As for her parents, Tom and Heidi, as well as her sister, Ada, your comments, encouragement, and inspiring ideas have helped me create what you now hold in your hands. I cherish your friendship.

Although the list is too long, I am especially grateful to the people of French River, Prince Edward Island for providing me with endless ideas and possibilities, as well as a setting that is simply breathtaking. Your generous spirit and lively storytelling have left their mark. We miss you enormously whenever we have to leave.

And thank you David Macleod, for taking care of Just Peachy, but more importantly, for being a good friend. "Toodly-doo" to you too!

I would also like to extend a huge thank-you to my dedicated editor, Grenfell Featherstone, who helped me shape *Secrets of the Dunes* into this exceptional little book. The hard work and sage advice is greatly appreciated and will be definitely put to good use in the future.

About the Author

Julianna Kozma's debut novel, *Mosquitoes of Summer*, was the 2009 winner of Book Idol. Julianna worked as a financial journalist before becoming a teacher. She divides her time between the Laurentians in Quebec and Prince Edward Island with her husband, their two children, and pet parrot, Mr. Bean.

Don't miss Hannah and Emily's
first fun-filled adventure!

Mosquitoes of Summer

The battered hull of a mysterious old ship washes
up on the beach near historic French River, Prince
Edward Island. Where did it come from? What
secrets lie hidden within? Perhaps pirate gold!
Hannah and Emily, two quirky sisters vacationing
on the island, decide to investigate. Set amid the
breathtaking scenery that has made this tiny
Canadian island such a popular tourist attraction,
Mosquitoes of Summer takes the reader from
one zany adventure to another.

Join Hannah and her gang of friends as they search
for clues in an abandoned graveyard, experience
the unfortunate pitfalls of buying a rundown
cottage, and face the tragic consequences of a
powerful coastal storm. Add a dose of ghost
stories and pirate lore and the result is an
unforgettable summer of hilarity.

NOW AVAILABLE IN PAPERBACK AND EBOOK